KALAM'S Family Tree

Ancestral Legacy of Dr. A.P.J. Abdul Kalam

KALAM'S
Family Tree

Ancestral Legacy of Dr. A.P.J. Abdul Kalam

DR. A. P. J. M. NAZEMA MARAIKAYAR

Translated by:
SRIPRIYA SRINIVASAN

PRABHAT
PRAKASHAN

Published by

PRABHAT PRAKASHAN PVT. LTD.
4/19 Asaf Ali Road,
New Delhi-110 002 (INDIA)
e-mail: prabhatbooks@gmail.com

ISBN 978-93-5562-812-1

KALAM'S FAMILY TREE: ANCESTRAL LEGACY OF DR. A.P.J. ABDUL KALAM
Dr. A. P. J. M. Nazema Maraikayar

Edition
2025

Price
₹ 300 (Rupees Three Hundred only)

Printed at
Yash Printographics, Noida

Foreword

I personally know about the scholarship of the author of this book. We became family friends through the former Indian President Dr. A. P. J. Abdul Kalam. Myself and Kalam's elder brother (Late) Mohammed Muthu Meera Lebbai Maraikayar were thick friends!

Mr. Maraikayar knew well about different herbs and their applications. He used to talk about the different plants and shrubs inside Rashtrapati Bhavan, and their medicinal qualities. I had asked Nazema to capture his knowledge in a book.

Nazema is the first member in her family to get a doctorate degree. In consultation with her father, she brought out a small book on herbal treatment in 2005.

Nine years after that, Nazema has now written this book 'Kalam's Family Tree' that talks about the story of their ancestors. She has also included present day incidents in this book. She has listened to these stories from her father and other members of her family. In this book these incidents appear as a narrative by her father to his grandson's granddaughter Hanija, which in itself is a new style of storytelling. The author also gives an opportunity to Hanija's mom to listen to these stories.

Hence, she has taken the initiative of helping two members from the present generation to understand past incidents without losing briskness in her narrative.

The initials A, P, J which appear in the name of the world famous scientist Dr. A. P. J. Abdul Kalam is the first letter of three of the senior most members of his family.

Nazema has not just written her family story here. She has also presented historical facts, societal changes, world war, ration and so on. News about 'Katchatheevu' has also been presented in this book.

The childhood pranks of the boy Abdul Kalam have also been furnished here.

The women in this large family tree share a status equivalent to that of its male members and their characters shine with brilliance.

This book is a tiny historic work which has presented the true story of a huge family tree.

I hope that Hajiya Dr. A. P. J. M. Nazema Maraikayar will publish books related to trees, shrubs, and plants soon.

With prayers to the Almighty...

– Dr. Y. S. Rajan
Honorary Distinguished Professor,
ISRO, Bengaluru,
Chairman, Board of Governors,
National Institute of Technology, Manipur.

Author's Note

This is the story about my ancestors till present date: I am thankful to my father's younger brother Dr. A. P. J. Abdul Kalam for asking me to compile a book about my ancestors by gathering information from my father A. P. J. M. Maraikayar!

I am thankful to my friend Dr. Y. S. Rajan who has always insisted that I should keep writing diligently so that my books are published and made available to one and all!

My blessings to my darlings Sheikh Dawood, Sheikh Saleem, and Meheraj Banu for bringing out this book in a printable format!

My good wishes to Mr. K. C. Rajkumar, Micro Computer Zone, for editing this book!

– Dr. A. P. J. M. Nazema Maraikayar

Translator's Note

Soon after my English translation of the life story of Kalam, "Memories Never Die: Dr. APJ Abdul Kalam" got published, I received a special request from Dr. Nazema Maraikayar madam. She wanted to check if I would be able to translate the book about Kalam's Family Tree from Tamil into English. I agreed.

As a student of philosophy and religion, I got to learn so much from this book about Islamic traditions and rituals. Along with the incidents that happened in the Maraikayar family, Dr. Nazema Maraikayar has also presented several historical facts in her narrative that makes the book appealing for inquisitive readers. Dr. Nazema Maraikayar thoroughly reviewed my translation and offered her invaluable feedback.

I feel fortunate to have not only translated Kalam's life story in my earlier book but also the story of his family tree in this present work. I am grateful to Dr. Nazema Maraikayar madam and other family members of Dr. Abdul Kalam for giving me this wonderful opportunity.

– Sripriya Srinivasan

October 15, 2023

Aerial Roots

Aerial Root - 1

Today is very special, for it is the birthday of Avul Pakir Jainulabdeen Abdul Kalam! He became famous for his contribution in the fields of defence and space technologies; he visited Switzerland on May 26, 2005; in order to commemorate his arrival, the Swiss government announced that May 26th will be known as 'Science Day' and honoured him. The news continued on TV...

Little Hanija who had curled like a tiny kitten on her small chair shouted Avul, Pakir, Jainulabdeen, Abdul Kalam... and jumped out of her seat. She asked her mother who was passing by, "Mom, isn't he our grandfather?" "Who, Hanija?" her mom asked back. Raising her eyebrows, Hanija replied to her mom, "Since yesterday everyone has been saying that it is the birthday of A. P. J. Abdul Kalam, right?... well, I know Abdul Kalam... but who are Avul, Pakir and the others...?"

Hanija's mom too wanted to know about all of them! "Hani, we shall go and meet our great grandfather in the evening. We will find out from him then. Now, please leave me alone for sometime." Saying so, she escaped from the multiple questions that her daughter was shooting at her.

Her great grandfather greeted them in the evening, "Come in!" Hanija's mother told him, "Your grandson's granddaughter is asking so many questions. You please answer her." She then told him that Hanija had asked her about Avul, Pakir, Jainulabdeen... He replied, "All these are our ancestors." "Please could you tell us about all of them?" asked Hanija's mom.

A. P. J. M. Maraikayar started narrating their family story to Hanija and her mom. He was the eldest son of Avul Pakir Jainulabdeen as well as the eldest brother of Dr. A. P. J. Abdul Kalam. This 97-year-old man went down the memory lane and started narrating their family story... He said, "Hanimma, let's first start from Avul, Okay?..."

'Avul Ambalam' - He wouldn't have known back then that this name would be the first name in a lengthy lineage. Isn't 'A' the first letter among the English alphabets? Even as I utter the word 'Ambalam', I can visualise a hefty person seated in an assembly and instructing people. The very word 'Ambalam' denotes his place as the village head who actively took part in the proceedings of their hometown, mingling hand-in-hand with the local people, doesn't it? He would prescribe the do's and don'ts to the townsmen and they too would listen to his advice sincerely back then! (in the 1700s)

It was not just Rameswaram town. It also included villages to the north like Mangaadu, Samba, Olaikuda, Sudu Kattampatti, Narikuzhi, Thaazhaiyadi, Vadakaadu,

Pillai Kulam, Ariyaangundu, Yerakaadu, Kudiyiruppu, and Semmamadam as well as villages to the west like Dheetchatharkollai and Nochivaadi, and those to the south like Karaiyur village. All these came under the overlordship of Ambalam.

Avul Ambalam's younger brother Ibrahim Ambalam had huge respect and regards for his brother. Out of respect for his brother's wife, he would stand up and greet her as 'Machi'. He helped his brother in taking care of their agricultural land and other property. He would roam about on land and in the sea as well to take care of their sea trade activities. Avul Ambalam and his brother were the owners of huge portions of land filled with coconut and palm trees. Coconuts and palm plantations were their source of living.

By maintaining these plantations carefully, they would sell coconuts from these trees in order to make a living. The products from palm trees such as tuber, leaves, and tender palmyra fruits also yielded good profit. They also owned tamarind plantations in places like Meyyampuli, Samba, and Yerakaadu. After taking some tamarind for their household use and for gifting, the rest of it was sold in the market.

The Ambalams had jobs on the seashore as well. They built boats out of wooden planks that would be used to seat people. Thus, they were sea traders as well. Since time immemorial, people would sail to and fro from Talaimannar and Dhanushkodi situated in Sri Lanka and

India respectively. Those from Talaimannar would get their tickets from the 'Vidhaanai' (government official in Sri Lanka) and after entering Dhanushkodi, they would hand over the tickets to the Headman (government official in India) there. Boats too had captains. They were known as 'Thandaiyal'. He was in-charge of sea travel. The boatmen would carry passengers on sailboats to Talaimannar and after dropping them there, they would return back with passengers to Dhanushkodi. Thus, by maintaining these boats and giving wages to the boatmen, the Ambalams ruled over the sea as well.

The Ambalams also maintained cattle in their sheds. In order to identify the owner of the cattle, they had imprinted the name 'Kathija' who was the wife of Avul Ambalam on the body of the cattle. On the exterior portion of their hindlimbs, the anchor symbol was engraved to indicate that they belonged to boat owners.

"Year after year these cows give birth to several calves and are brought to our home. We get huge quantities of milk, buttermilk, and ghee from them. By heating the butter made out of their milk, we get ghee which we use along with rice and other food items. There is never a shortage of these milk products in our home!" The family members of the Ambalams boasted like this.

The milk-yielding cows were stationed in mangrove watersheds and built-in watersheds. They were fed with water and grass in these places. The watersheds in which water tasted and smelt as sweet as mangoes were known as mangrove watersheds and these were on the outskirts of the city. The built-in watersheds were the ones that stored water in square, long square, and rectangular layouts.

Even after several years of marriage, Avul Ambalam was not blessed with children. This distressed the family members. After repeated prayers, with the Grace of God, they were blessed with a baby boy. Their relatives and friends rejoiced at the birth of 'Pakir Meera Lebbai Ambalam'. Thc townsfolk felt happy that the next Ambalam had arrived.

At a young age, this little boy learnt the Qur'an as well as the Tamil alphabets. He would address Avul Ambalam as 'Vaappa' and Ibrahim Ambalam as 'Chinnaappa'. Ibrahim Ambalam was very fond of the child. Be it the plantations or the seashore, he would carry the child on his shoulders wherever he went.

Every morning began with the call for the 'Fajr' prayer during which 'Allahu Akbar' (God is Great) would be recited. Wearing his wooden sandals, Ambalam went to pray in the local mosque even before the break of dawn. People greeted him with 'Assalamu Alaikum' (Let peace prevail upon you!) and he would greet them back saying 'Wa Alaikum Salam' and climb up the stairs.

After his prayers, his daily routine would start. He walked swiftly in the southern direction. Everyone greeted him on the way. Smiling and greeting them back, he hurried.

The coconut trees welcomed him by shaking their branches. "The boss is here!" someone shouted. "Hey Chinnaan, have you plucked the coconuts?" Ambalam asked him. "Yes sir. Roughly about three hundred coconuts. Now I am going to take out their outer shells!" Saying so, Chinnaan started to remove the coconut shells with his sickle.

Next, Ambalam visited the palm plantation. Over there, Periyasamy was cutting the young palmyra fruits. He was Chinnaan's elder brother's son. Hearing the noise coming from Ambalam's stick, he raised his head. "Please come, sir. Our Vella Mandi Nadaar asked for palm splints", he said. "Send him whatever he wants. Don't ask him for money", Ambalam replied. Such was the value of their friendship! "Go and give some young palmyra fruits to people in my home", Ambalam ordered. Judging the time of the day by looking at the sun, he then walked home. The door opened and there stood his wife Kathija Nachiyar in a beautiful blue Koranad silk saree. She greeted her husband warmly.

"Will you bathe now?" she asked him. She was of average height, slightly plump with a fair complexion and a sharp nose. "The coconuts and palmyra fruits were delivered", she announced. After removing his towel from his shoulder and handing it out to her, Ambalam removed his dhoti and went to take his bath. Soothing warm water was kept ready in a huge brass vessel in the backyard. After bathing, he did his 'Wudu' (Personal hygiene is very important for the prayer ritual. So, one has to do Wudu before praying. Wudu includes washing one's face and hands, scrubbing the hair on one's head with wet hands, and washing the legs.) After this, he sat on his prayer mat facing the west to do his Nafl prayer. (Other than the five-times-daily prayer ritual and excluding those times allotted for personal special prayers, one can perform the Nafl prayer). After praying, he said Alhamdullillah and sat down on his palm mat. Kathija Nachiyar served him hot idiyappam with coconut milk and sugar in porcelain plates and brought a brass tumbler filled with lukewarm water.

Even before he could finish his food, someone shouted from outside, "Kaakka, Kaakka..." Two people involved in a field dispute wanted to meet him to settle the fight. After enquiring about the quarrel, Ambalam told them that he would come the next day to personally see their respective agricultural lands and then give a solution. He then rested on his easychair for a while.

"We have come to invite you for a wedding." A few people from the Paradava clan had come to invite him. "You must definitely attend it, sir", they said while leaving. The entire hall smelt of turmeric and sandalwood.

As he heard the call for the 'Dhuhr' prayer, Ambalam walked to the mosque. After he came back, his wife Kathija Nachiyar served him cooked parboiled rice with fish gravy and drumstick leaves gravy. She then brought the betelnut box for him.

She politely offered the betel leaves with lime and betel nuts to Ambalam and said, "We must look for an alliance for your brother. A good one has come from the third house. The girl is Meera Naina's elder brother's daughter." Munching his betel leaves, he said, "Okay, let's do it!" Delighted with his response, Kathija Nachiyar went in to have her lunch. Ambalam rested for a while. Soon, it was teatime. Kathija Nachiyar took a jar and went to the cowshed and collected some milk from one of the cows for the tea. The other cows mooed.

The maid servant Sulaihamma opened the back door for Muthu in order to milk the cows. Huge quantities of milk in large vessels were collected by him, after which, he received some fresh palmyra fruits for his services from Nachiyar and left the house.

Ambalam had finished drinking his tea. Now, it was time for the afternoon 'Asr' prayer. After finishing his prayer at the mosque, he sat there for sometime. Since he was the Mutawalli (ancestral head of governors of the mosque), he wanted to cross-check the account transactions of the mosque.

As it was the beginning of the month, he gave salary to 'Pesh Imam' who conducted the five-times-a-day prayer ritual at the mosque. He then gave salary to 'Modhinaar' who was in-charge of rendering Adhan, cleaning the mosque, and helping the local townsmen in times of need. Two people who were quarrelling amongst themselves appeared in front of him. Ambalam resolved their fight by saying, “The Prophet has preached us peace and harmony. Why are you two fighting like this then?” He made them salute and hug (‘Musafahah’) each other.

It was now time for the evening ‘Maghrib’ prayer. Ambalam, who was already sitting outside the mosque, went in to perform his prayer. He then returned back home, where his friend Naadar was waiting for him. The two friends lost track of time. The call for the night time ‘Isha’ prayer was heard and Ambalam went to the mosque to pray. When he returned home for dinner, hot Rava Upma was served. He then had some bananas and milk. He then strolled inside the house for sometime.

“Meera Naina’s brother is here”, announced Kathija Nachiyar. He formally greeted him by saying ‘Assalam Alaikum’ and sat down to discuss the marriage proposal. The wedding date for Ibrahim-Alima Beevi’s marriage was fixed. Their house buzzed with the marriage arrangements. The entire town gathered to attend the wedding celebration. Musical instruments like Nadhaswaram and drums reverberated through the hall. The wedding went smoothly. Everyone rejoiced since it was the wedding function in their boss’s family. For about one week to ten days, the local people were celebrating the wedding.

After the celebrations, Ambalam marched towards their Karaiyur plantation. A few people approached him and saluted. They looked perplexed. They were in-charge of town cleaning. Even before he could ask for the reason, Rakki appeared before him.

"Sir, we are living like nomads. Please give us a place to reside. May you live like a king!", she said. Ambalam told them, "Alright, you all come see me tomorrow." He was looking for a solution. After returning home, he called out to his wife Kathija Nachiyar. "Our Rakki wanted a place for her people to live in. We have some patta lands to the north and east, right? I am planning to give them those lands", he told her. "Allah has blessed us well. It is because of them that our house and plantations are clean. You give them the land", said his beloved wife.

The cleaners settled down in the land allotted for them. They installed a few huts over there. The place came to be known as 'Sakkiliyar Residence'. The residents of the land showered their love and affection towards Ambalam and his family for giving them a permanent place to reside.

Contemplating over something, Ambalam entered the Habil-Qabil Dargah. Habil and Qabil were the sons of the first Prophet Adam. Habil and Qabil were buried inside this Dargah. As it was quite close to their plantations, the Ambalams frequently visited the Dargah. Ambalam was thinking about what his mother had told him about the Habil-Qabil Dargah. Habil and Qabil were the sons of the first forefather of mankind Adam, and Eve. They fought with each other on account of some misunderstanding. During the course of the fight, one of them lost his life.

The other one was petrified. Just then, two crows were fighting with each other. One of them fell down dead. The other crow buried the dead one. After digging the ground with its beak, it brought some water to cleanse the dead crow. It then covered it with a small piece of cloth. After praying to God, it buried the dead crow inside the ground and flew away with a heavy heart and with tears pouring out of its eyes. After watching the bird, Qabil buried his dead brother Habil in a similar fashion. He was roaming around for sometime in that place and died soon after.

A local shepherd boy found the idol of a God on the seashore. The boy worshipped the idol earnestly. He prayed affectionately. Later on, many people started to worship the idol. A small temple was built around it. Later on, a bigger temple was erected in the place.

One of the ancestors of the Ambalam brothers had a dream: "Both of us- Habil and Qabil- were buried close to the place where the temple is constructed. We wish to reside on the outskirts of this city. You will find some lemons on the southern corner of your plantation. Please bury us over there."

The next day when he went and saw, their ancestor spotted lemon trees extending far and wide in that area. He constructed tombs for them in that same place. He then covered the roof and made it into a Dargah. A golden flag is erected in the Ramaswamy temple to honour Habil and Qabil.

These could perhaps be tales spread by people who wished for peace and harmony in the land. The story of Habil and Qabil appears in the chapter al-Ma'idah in the Holy Qur'an (verses 27-31). Here it is mentioned how Allah sent a crow that dug up the ground and demonstrated how to bury a dead one to Qabil. Therein, under chapter 5, section 6, it is mentioned that Habil and Qabil were the sons of Adam and how they faced their death. In fond memory of Habil, Ambalam was named as Avul.

After reciting the Al-Fatiha in the Habil-Qabil Dargah, Ambalam went to the mosque for his night time 'Isha' prayer. He then returned home, had his tiffin, and saying 'Al-Hamdulillah' he went to sleep. Suddenly, he woke up asking for his brother. "Where is Ibrahim?" His wife replied, "He must be in the shop only." "Oh! The paddy grains must have arrived", said Ambalam. There were two shops owned by Avul Ambalam and Ibrahim Ambalam in the eastern street. They sent boats to the seashore in Thondi to procure the paddy bundles. They then sold these grains in their shops. In those days, people would buy paddy, then by beating them would prepare rice out of them.

In a short while, Ibrahim Ambalam returned home with his brother's son. They both washed their hands and legs and sat down for dinner. Under the hurricane lamp light, they then discussed the profit and loss incurred through the procurement of paddy grains, sale of coconuts, split palmyra and acacias.

"Our Peer Kaakaa's daughter is getting married", Ibrahim told his brother. "Please give them one sack of paddy on our behalf", said Avul Ambalam. Looking at the generosity of the two brothers, the women who were sitting inside felt very happy.

As he was about to sleep, Avul Ambalam asked for his son Pakir. "He slept already", replied his wife Nachiyar. "Remember to wake him up at 5 o'clock tomorrow morning for prayer", Ambalam instructed her. Nachiyar knew that prayer was mandatory at the age of seven. However, out of affection for her son, she said, "Isn't he a little child?" to which Ambalam replied sharply, "This little child will become big one day. Good habits must be cultivated at a young age. Don't forget to wake him up in the morning."

At the break of dawn, listening to the call for prayer, Kathija Nachiyar remembered her husband's instructions and woke her son up. She gave him some homemade tooth powder, made him perform the Wudu ritual, and sent him with his father for the morning prayer to the mosque.

Thus began Pakir's first day of the Holy Qur'an recitation. Nachiyar served tea to her husband, brother-in-law and son. Then, Pakir was sent to the mosque to learn the letters of the Holy Qur'an from Pesh Imam. (It was customary to recite the Holy Qur'an on one side of the mosque. Pesh Imam taught the children to write the letters of the Holy Qur'an in a place known as Halaqat al-ilm (Halaqa in short or Halka according to the new edition of the encyclopaedia of Islam). For breakfast, Kathija Nachiyar decided to make puttu (a form of loose pudding variety) out of the ragi given by Velaayi the previous day. She asked her brother-in-law's wife Alima Beevi to bring the ragi flour and prepared delicious puttu by adding some ghee, sugar and grated coconut to it.

It was the time for the Ramanathaswamy temple idol procession. The entire town was buzzing with activity. People were celebrating all over the place. Children were excited. Traders and merchants from several places had camped there. The central attraction was the float festival. People gathered in large numbers to witness the event. The idols of Ramanathaswamy and his consort Parvatavardini Ambal marched jubilantly during the float festival procession. Suddenly, the idols fell into the water and submerged. People who witnessed this were flabbergasted. They didn't know what to do! Each one was suggesting some solution to recover the idols from the water.

This news reached Ambalam who was having his dinner. Immediately, he summoned a few boatmen and fishermen. He went along with them to the spot and ordered them to dive in to recover the idols. Straw Effigies were lit up to get some light. The search was on...

Their efforts didn't go for a waste. One after another, the submerged idols were recovered by them. They started swimming towards the shore. They handed over the idols to Ambalam who was standing perplexed there with a white turban over his head. "Ya Allah!" Ambalam thanked God's mercy. He then handed over the idols along with all other materials that got submerged to the temple authorities.

When Avul Ambalam returned home with his brother, it was already past midnight. The people gathered around dispersed happily.

"Alright! Come, let's all go to my house", said Ambalam to the fishermen and boatmen who had helped recover the idols. Everyone followed him. He brought some fresh dhotis from inside his house for them. He saw that his brother too had brought some dhotis for them.

The workers replied shyly, "It's alright, sir. Our dhotis will dry in the air soon." Ambalam replied, "It's fine. Please take these to wear. You all may sleep outside our house tonight." They thanked him for his kind gesture.

The door opened. Ibrahim Ambalam had brought some rice soaked in water, fish gravy in two large vessels and some water in a huge brass vessel to feed the workers. They slept peacefully outside the house. The next morning, without disturbing their sleep, Ambalam went to the mosque to pray. When he returned, they were already awake. He asked them to stay for a while and went inside the house. He brought some money. He then called out to Muniyaandi and told him, "All of you use this to feed yourselves." They then returned to their homes.

Looking at the time, he proceeded to his plantation. Suddenly, he changed his mind and proceeded to the seashore instead and purchased a huge fish and called out to one of his workers. "Chinnaan! Hand this in the house", he instructed him. He spent some time with his workers and then left for Keppai Vaadi." (Keppai Vaadi belonged to the Ambalams. Ragi was planted here, harvested and sealed inside sack bags. It was then beaten and nearly some 300 measures of ragi were distributed to their relatives, friends and workers every year after they used some for their household use.) He inspected the ragi that was ready to harvest. He instructed Kamatchiappan who was in-charge, "You take the help from a few people and harvest these this Sunday." He left home. He left his wooden sandals outside the house. (They used these wooden sandals while going to their plantation to avoid hard stones and thorns on the way. They measured their leg size in the shop and instructed the cobbler to stitch fittingly along with a small rope and nails.)

Looking at the tired face of his brother Ibrahim Ambalam, he enquired, "What happened, Ibrahim?" Ibrahim suffered from fever. He then called out to his wife Kathija. "My brother has a fever", he said. "I am preparing a decoction to cure him", she replied. Meanwhile, Chinnaan had returned with the fish. He called out to him, "Sir..." "Ok, you go to our plantation in the east..." Even as he was saying this, Kaali entered with fresh arrow roots. "Periyamma had asked the milkman Muthu to gather these to cure our little sir's illness", Kaali said.

After taking the arrowroots from Kaali, Avul Ambalam handed over two annas to him from his wallet. Kaali left. He took the fish from Chinnaan and went inside thinking... 'How affectionate Kathija is towards her brother-in-law! It is only when the women of the house take good care of the household, can the men perform well outside without any worries!' He handed over the arrow roots and the fish to Kathija Nachiyar. Looking at her husband, she asked, "What's the matter?" "Even as I was about to suggest bringing arrow roots, they had already arrived", Ambalam replied thankfully. (In order to prepare the decoction, arrow roots were boiled with herbs like pepper, galangal and long pepper in an earthen pot with a glass of water. Once the water reduced to a quarter portion, the mixture was filtered, mixed with some powdered jaggery and served.)

Understanding her husband fully well, Kathija Nachiyar replied, "If there is fever, we need to serve herbal decoction, right? Alright, now you go for your bath." After bathing in the soothing warm water, Ambalam did the Wudu ritual, recited the Nafl prayer and sat down to have his food.

Kathija Nachiyar brought hot milk Kozhukattai in a porcelain bowl and served him. "Since your brother was ill, we thought of making this. It would be tasty for him", she said. Ambalam thought to himself... 'Is this the only reason, or is she praising me for recovering the submerged idols'. Thinking thus, he smiled to himself.

Whatever be the reason, the Kozhukattai tasted delicious. People from the temple authorities called to him from outside, "Sir..." They had brought some flowers, betel leaves, and fruits in a big plate in order to thank him. The team was headed by the temple administrative officer Sastrigal and Ganapaadigal. Ramachandra Sastri, who was very old, thanked Ambalam profusely, "You have helped us hugely, sir", and handed over the plate to him. "There should be no such formalities between us", Ambalam said and asked them to be seated.

"We have arranged for a meeting in the Devasthanam Matam in the evening. You must definitely come there", said the temple administrative officer. Ambalam agreed. Everyone left. The entire house was filled with the fragrance of fresh flowers and fruits. After finishing his afternoon 'Dhuhr' prayer, he came home for lunch. Pepper kuzhambu was prepared with the fish. "This pepper gravy is to cure my brother's illness, right?" he asked and began to eat. When he woke up from his nap, he could smell the arrow root decoction.

After he finished his 'Asr' prayer at the mosque, he went to the Matam. Those in-charge of the temple administration were waiting for him over there. They all welcomed him and offered him a seat. They said that they had completed the remedial rituals since the idols got submerged the previous night. They were perplexed at what had happened on the previous night. They were discussing how to avoid such mishaps in the future. Ambalam offered his suggestion. He said that they could tie them all to a wooden plank securely and then perform the float festival.

Everyone agreed to his suggestion. They asked Ambalam to take care of the necessary arrangements. Ambalam said that God Willing, he would make the same efforts for the next year's float festival. He returned home. He was thinking of how to execute it on his way back home. As soon as he entered, he searched for his brother. Ibrahim Ambalam was seated facing east, with the decoction in his hand.

As he tried to get up, Avul Ambalam asked him to be seated and enquired, "Have you had your decoction?" Ibrahim said, "Yes", and kept his tumbler upside down in a corner and sat at a distance after finishing it. "Aren't you thinking that your brother-in-law lacks digestion and that's why he has seated himself at a distance?" he asked his wife. It was customary to keep the decoction cup upside down after drinking, and to move away from the place where one was seated while drinking it. Ambalam was wondering why people did that... *The cup with the decoction smelt of the arrowroot essence. Since it shouldn't be used for other cooking purposes, they probably did this...* he thought to himself.

*Also, if one sits in the same place after drinking the decoction, he could face indigestion problems. It is always better to stroll a little and be seated elsewhere...*he thought. He rushed to the mosque as he heard the call for the 'Maghrib' prayer. He checked if the lamps had enough oil in them. He lost track of time. Modhinaar called out for the 'Isha' prayer. He closed his Holy Qur'an book and got ready to pray.

He came home, had his dinner and slept. Time flew. The days and nights were filled with happiness, sorrow, anger and peace. It was now time for the annual float festival. As promised earlier, Ambalam got busy in constructing the boat for the festival. He called out to his boatmen. He gave them a rough sketch of the boat and asked for their opinion. They all approved happily.

They decided to tie six fishing boats together, attach them to a bamboo support from beneath and to fix wooden planks on top to construct the boat for the float festival. The festival began. A huge crowd gathered around the temple tanks of Rama and Lakshmana. The boat was constructed as per Ambalam's suggestion. Two men stationed inside the Lakshmana tank held ropes attached to the boat.

The other end of the rope was held by two men from Karaiyur seashore in Rameswaram. They had stationed themselves on the stairs of the water tank. Rama Naamavali was recited all around. Inside the boat, the priests recited the Vedas and were performing the pooja rituals. They sat under the feet of the idols of Ramanathaswamy and Parvatavardini Ambal. The tank was lit up with lights and the whole place reverberated with sacred hymns of God. People were immersed in this divine aura. The boat floated inside the water without any untoward incidents. The festival started at around 8 PM. Children witnessed the festival sitting on the laps of their moms. They watched this beautiful festival without blinking. As time passed, they began to sleep.

The boat made nine rounds. People happily returned home with things they had purchased during the festivity. Crackers were burst to celebrate the success of the festival. The Gods were stationed in the northern Mandapam of the temple tank. The place echoed with the sound 'Harahara'. Avul Ambalam and his brother Ibrahim Ambalam who were amidst their boatmen workers heaved a sigh of relief. The officials from the temple Devasthanam welcomed both of them.

As they reached the sanctum sanctorum, the Ambalams handed over the silk saree and silk uttariya (upper garment) specially bought for the occasion. After receiving these, the temple official honoured the Ambalam. He gave them a plate with three silk sarees, five dhotis, flowers, fruits, coconuts, and a silk cloth with money. With his worker retinue following him, the Ambalam went home. He handed over the silk sarees to his wife. He gave the dhotis to his workers. He then handed two-thirds of the money to his workers. They all left.

Ambalam felt happy that the float festival went on smoothly. Thanking God, he went to bed. The next day began with a prayer. After praying, the Ambalams went to their plantations and returned home. Soon after they had finished their food, someone called from outside.

"Are the Ambalams inside?" It was the people from the Ramanathaswamy temple Devasthanam. They had brought sacks of rice, vegetables, and prasadam from the temple to honour the Ambalam brothers. The head official praised them. Thanking them profusely, he requested them to be in-charge of constructing the boat for the float festival every year. After they left, Ambalam sent for his workers and distributed half of the rice to them. After taking a few vegetables, he distributed the rest as well as the kumkum and vibhuti prasadams to them. The workers were very happy to receive these.

One morning, Avul Ambalam woke up with a high fever. His eyes were burning, his tongue tasted bitterly. Somehow he finished his morning prayer ritual and had the tea prepared by his wife. Periyanaagan, the local doctor, was summoned. Periyanaagan was an efficient doctor. He knews very well the nature of flatulence, biliousness and phlegm that caused illness. He knew how to cure an illness through medicines and surgery as required. He also knew herbal treatments to cure medical ailments. He and his ancestors were medical practitioners, and they were the formal doctors for people like Ambalam since time immemorial. They were given a fixed amount of money, paddy, coconuts on a monthly basis. They also received clothes and other accessories annually as well as other materials as required in times of need. Naagan rushed to Ambalam's house. He confirmed that it was an ordinary fever and asked them to prepare a decoction as required. He asked Ambalam to drink some porridge before eating the tablets prescribed by him. He said that he would come back in the evening to see his progress.

Relatives rushed to his house to see Ambalam and enquire about his health. After drinking his porridge and consuming his medicines, Ambalam rested for a while. He thought of so many things.... The fact that his brother had no children haunted him foremost. He was woken up in the evening by his doctor. The fever had gone down and he started to sweat. The doctor was happy that his treatment had worked. He asked Ambalam to get some rest. Ibrahim Ambalam brought some coconuts and banana plantains and offered it to the doctor. After taking his bath in lukewarm water, Avul Ambalam was seated. He heard a commotion from outside. "We hope that you are doing well, sir." Two men from the Ramanathaswamy temple were standing. "It is time for Pongal, right?" Saying so, they placed the things they had brought with them in the hall. They filled the hall with pots meant for

Pongal, raw rice, turmeric tubers, sugarcane, jaggery, betel leaves, betel nuts and so on. The temple officials left. The boatmen in-charge of the float festival were summoned. Pongal pots filled with raw rice and other materials were handed out to them. Kathija Nachiyar distributed the leftover portion to her friends, relatives and neighbours. She had prepared pumpkin gravy for lunch. Soon after he recovered, Ambalam started to go to the mosque for his prayer routine. He also visited his plantations. He was glad that his brother had taken good care of their plantations while he was unwell. "Ya Allah! Please bless my brother with a child!" he prayed.

Days passed. Last few days of the month of Sha'ban was left. Then it would be time for Ramzan fasting. They ground raw rice in mortars and saved them in pots to prepare idiyappam. They fried parboiled rice and kept it ready to make suitable snacks. They prepared pickles out of lemons and citron. On the last day of Sha'ban, they gathered to celebrate. They had coconut rice with kurma for lunch. The little ones prepared food collectively with the help of their mothers in the bronze vessels given to them. They shared their food and ate happily.

The Ramadan moon was sighted. They greeted each other and got ready to observe Ramadan fasting. Call for the 'Taraweeh' prayer was heard from the Mohaideen Abdul Qadar Aandavar Mosque. (Taraweeh prayer is a special prayer observed from the day of sighting the moon in Ramadan until Eid (when Shawwal moon is sighted) right after the 'Isha' prayer at night.)

They slept a while after the Taraweeh prayer. They realised it was 3 AM, when they heard the songs from the Fakirs. (The Fakirs would carry a small drum in their hands while singing the glories of God, Prophets and the disciples. They would visit each and every house to receive whatever they give and bless the house. Their arrival during the fasting season would indicate that it was Sahur time. They usually lived as a community.) The Muslim people did the Wudu ritual and recited the Tahajjud prayer.

Kathija Nachiyar and Alima Beevi prepared idiyappam and kurma for Sahur. (Sahur Time is the time from late night until 4:30 AM. People who observed fasting should eat during this time.) Everyone in Ambalam's family, including his son Pakir, observed Sahur and took an oath to observe fasting during the month of Ramadan. As soon as he heard the prayer calls for the morning 'Fajr' prayer, Avul Ambalam rushed with his brother Ibrahim Ambalam and son Fakir to the mosque. During the fasting season, they spent their days and nights reciting the Holy Qur'an.

Whoever sought alms were given abundantly. Charitable deeds were performed. Those who sought food were given food. After the 'Asr' prayer, porridge was distributed in the mosque. In the evening, they broke their fact with a date fruit and drank the porridge. They then prayed to Allah:

"Ya Allah! I am observing this fast to you. I only believe in you. I shall now break my fast with your food." Saying so, they break their fast. Then as always, after the 'Maghrib' prayer, they ate rice fish gravy and some curry and took some rest. Next was the Taraweeh prayer... in this way they spent their fasting season thinking of Allah. Koranad silk sarees, and shirts were brought from the textile shop for the women of the household to select. Kathija Nachiyar and Alima Beevi selected a blue and a green saree.

They also gave away sarees, dhotis, and other dress materials to their workers and the poor people. The women of the household prepared 'Seepu Paniyaarams' and 'Achu Paniyaaram' for the big day. After thirty days, 'Shawwal' moon was sighted. The elders announced that they would celebrate Ramzan the following day since the 'Shawwal' moon was sighted.

The prayer timings for Ramzan were announced in the mosque. Everyone rejoiced and said 'Eid Mubarak!' Kathija Nachiyar's brother-in-law and his wife eagerly prepared some 'Wattalappam' to welcome the special day. They then prepared 'Velladai', and went to bed. They woke up at 4 AM. After praying, they ate some Wattalappam and Velladai. Wearing new clothes, they all went to the mosque to pray. Before going, Avul Ambalam gave his 'Pithra' to his family members. After finishing their prayer, Kathija Nachiyar and Alima Beevi packed the Paniyaarams in straw boxes and distributed them to their relatives. Avul Ambalam distributed sweets to his friends, Nadaar and recruiters. They gave away money and savouries to whoever asked from the front and back doors. The launderer Kandhan, barber Munisaamy, and cleaner Raakki took their money and savouries early in the morning and departed happily.

As days went by, Avul Ambalam was finding it difficult to roam around his plantations. He was feeling tired constantly. As he was finding difficulty breathing, he chanted *'La Ilaha Illallah Muhammadur Rasulullah'* (I bear witness that there is no deity but God, and I bear witness that Mohammad is the messenger of God - this is the first of the five Kalimas of Islam) and breathed his last. People who fondly addressed him as 'Ambalam' and 'Sir' had gathered there to witness his departure. Tears fell from the eyes of those whose disputes Avul Ambalam had settled.

He was a great man who was venerated by one and all in the society and a beloved member of his family. After the death of her husband, Kathija Nachiyar became silent. Alima Beevi comforted her. Ibrahim Ambalam hugged his nephew who had lost his beloved father and cried uncontrollably. Time flew. As they say, 'Time is the best healer.' Over time, God has given human beings the ability to forget the past and move on. Perhaps, it is this quality that helps them heal faster...

❑

Aerial Root - 2

Ibrahim Ambalam started filling up the place of his late brother by taking care of their plantations, gardens, boats, and so on. He carefully maintained each of these with utmost dedication. He sent his brother's son to study in a school. He taught him the recitation of the Holy Qur'an and other religious activities prescribed to Muslims. Days passed from summer to winter. It was now time for Diwali. On the day before Diwali, two people from the temple came to their house. They handed over some gingelly oil and shikakai powder on behalf of the temple management to Pakir who was passing by. The temple authorities continued to honour the Ambalam family as always.

One day, Alima Beevi was struck with fever. The usual herbal decoction had no effect on her. As her body temperature was rising up and going down, they summoned their family doctor. All of his herbal tablets, powders and oils couldn't cure her. Alima Beevi passed away one evening. Ibrahim Ambalam was heart-broken. Kathija Nachiyar couldn't bear the loss of Alima Beevi who was like her own dear sister to her. The thought of how Alima Beevi would help her with all the household activities and how she would follow her everywhere like a little pet kitten came to her. Days passed. On the fortieth day after the passing away of Alima Beevi, they recited verses from the Holy Qur'an, fed the poor and prayed for her soul to rest in peace. Relatives came with several marriage proposals to Ibrahim Ambalam for his second marriage. Kathija Nachiyar too was on the lookout for a suitable alliance for him.

Ibrahim Ambalam immersed himself in his daily routine, paying little attention to all these proposals. He did not want to marry again. He spent most of his time with his brother's son. Pakir was engaged in praying and learning. During the rest of the time, Ibrahim Ambalam would take Pakir to show him their plantations and other property. He would take him to the seashore and teach him about the nuances of their shipping and fishing industries. Ambalam was very particular that his nephew learnt to read and write well. He therefore brought teachers to their house to teach him. Pakir was an ardent learner.

As Pakir was approaching marriageable age, his mom and Ibrahim Ambalam were on the lookout for suitable proposals. Many of their relatives were ready to give their daughters in marriage to Pakir. After carefully analysing, they decided that Sultan Beevi Fathima, who was the eldest daughter of Avul Ambalam's friend and relative Seeni Naina Muhammad, was the ideal bride for their family. The marriage of Pakir Maraikayar with Sultan Beevi

Fathima was announced all over the town. With the Grace of God Almighty, their wedding went smoothly. With the blessings of their friends and relatives, Avul Ambalam's son's wedding happened jubilantly. Pakir's mom and his uncle Ibrahim Ambalam were happy that they had fulfilled their duty well.

Sultan Beevi Fathima entered the newly painted house of Avul Ambalam and his family as their bride. She was fair and a little plump. She would help her mother-in-law Kathija Nachiyar in all the household chores. Several days went by. Pakir Ambalam was engaged in taking care of their properties along with Ibrahim Ambalam. They grew cows and sheep in large numbers. The Ambalam family flourished with all their properties and livestock.

Relatives were delighted to hear news of Sultan Beevi Fathima's pregnancy. Her mother-in-law Kathija Nachiyar and uncle Ibrahim Ambalam took very good care of her. The progeny of the Ambalam family was growing inside her. Mangoes and lemons were brought in huge quantities and made into pickles. Kathija Nachiyar would happily prepare whatever her daughter-in-law wanted during her pregnancy. Her parents came to take her to their house during the seventh month of pregnancy. Kathija Nachiyar told them that she would send her to their house after the 'Maghrib' prayer. The men of the household returned home after their everyday routine inspection of the plantations and the dockyard.

The girl's parents and relatives came to take her home. They brought some betel leaves, betel nuts, and fruits as a mark of auspiciousness. Kathija Nachiyar prepared tea for them. She then asked her daughter-in-law to wear a silk saree, and handed over some silver coins kept inside betel leaves to mark the occasion. Ibrahim Ambalam prayed to God Almighty to bless their family. He said, "Have a safe delivery and come back", to Sultan Beevi Fathima.

Waving her goodbye to her husband Pakir, Sultan Beevi Fathima went to her home for delivery. She was accompanied by their relatives. As soon as she entered, her sisters Havva Ammal, Mariyammal, Ayishamma, and Alimamma hugged her tightly. Her brother Mohammad Meera Lebbai Maraikayar who was fondly known as 'Sahib Maraikka' greeted her with a smile. They served tasty coconut rice, idiyappam and kari kurma to Pakir's relatives and little children who had accompanied their girl.

Everyone waited eagerly for the arrival of the little one. During the ninth month of pregnancy, rice soaked in milk was distributed among their relatives. Kathija Nachiyar informed her daughter-in-law's family that she would prepare Sool Paniyaram and bring them. With the help of her lady relatives, she prepared Seepu Paniyaram and Athirasam and packed them neatly in straw boxes. Together with banana plantains, betel leaves, betel nuts, and flowers, she visited her daughter-in-law. She enquired about her well-being, drank the tea prepared by Sultan Beevi Fathima's mom and after conversing a little with all of them, headed back home. In order to announce to their relatives that Sultan Beevi Fathima had come to her parents' home for delivery, they prepared 'Kathu Kanji' (a type of porridge) and distributed it to their relatives.

In the evenings, their lady relatives would flock into their house with loads of delicious snacks and savouries that they had prepared affectionately for Sultan Beevi Fathima. Their family would later distribute these delicacies to their neighbours and friends. Whenever she had some time, Kathija Nachiyar would make a visit to see her daughter-in-law Sultan Beevi Fathima. After Pakir completed his everyday routine and did his 'Isha' Prayer, she would send some delicious snacks through her son to her daughter-in-law. Pakir would enter his father-in-law's house shyly. He would then hand over the snacks to his wife who greeted him with a smile.

As soon as she heard that her daughter-in-law was going through labour pain, Kathija Nachiyar rushed faster than the wind. Lady physicians (midwife) who took care of the delivery were summoned. In the morning, a baby girl was born. The entire family was happy to hear this news. When Pakir heard the good news, he planted more coconuts and palms in his plantations in Karaiyur and expanded their family property. The local people over there warmly greeted him as their brother, son, and son-in-law. On special occasions, the ladies from Karaiyur would extend a helping hand in the chores of the Ambalam family.

It was the naming ceremony of Pakir Ambalam's daughter on the fortieth day. Sultan Beevi Fathima's dad's house was decorated for the occasion. Close relatives were invited. Sugar-candy, dates, bananas, pomegranates and other fruits were kept on plates. Pesh Imam prayed to God Almighty and named the silk-clad little baby who was sitting on Ibrahim Ambalam's lap as 'Seinambu Nachiyar.'

Kathija Nachiyar presented the baby with a gold chain. Those in Sultan Beevi Fathima's house presented the little one with golden bangles. Tiny little rings decorated the tiny little fingers of the baby. As everyone started petting her child, Sultan Beevi Fathima was worried that the little one might become uneasy. Kathija Nachiyar who understood the feelings of her daughter-in-law brought the little one to her mother and seated her on her lap. The baby fell asleep. At the end of the week, Kathija Nachiyar along with a few lady relatives went to her daughter-in-law's house to bring her and the little one back to their home. "We need to call Avvakkar to install the cradle for the child", she said and the boy was summoned. Abu Baker was his name. He was slightly taller than the average height. "Did you call me, aunty?" he enquired. After seeing the baby, he started to install the rope for the cradle.

Abu Baker chose the right ceiling for the baby cradle. He carefully connected a rope in order to attach the cradle bed. Kathija Nachiyar tied a white cloth to the rope he had fixed and prepared the cradle bed for the little one. She then gave some sugar-candy and fruits to Abu Baker and enquired about his mother as he left. They did not allow male members to enter into the inner premises of their house even if they were close relatives. However, an exception was made for Abu Baker. He was the son of their neighbour Chinnakkani Ravuthar- Seeniamma couple. He was also very dear to Saligu Lebbai whom Seeniamma married after Chinnakkani Ravuthar's demise.

Abu Baker used to roam inside Ambalam's house freely even from his childhood days. He had gained their love and affection from a very young age and was very dear to all of them. Salibu Lebbai trained him to recite the Holy Qur'an and taught him all religious activities pertaining to Islam. He grew up to be a good lad. Since Kathija Nachiyar treated him as a son belonging to their own family, she sought his help in tying the rope for the cradle. The arrival of the new born brought happiness to the family members. They changed their daily routine to suit the sleep cycle of the baby. While she was awake, the baby was on her granny's lap all the time. Little Seinambu started to speak aaa, ooo and so on in her tender voice. She started crawling, and then she slowly began to walk.

Kathija Nachiyar's health deteriorated over time. Her body temperature was wavering. The medicines given by the doctor could not cure her. She died by the end of the month. The entire family mourned the death of that great lady who was like a great pillar of support to all of them. Sultan Beevi Fathima became very depressed at the loss of her mother-in-law who constantly helped her in taking care of her baby. The family burden increased. Sultan Beevi Fathima helped the male members of the family during the recitation of the Holy Qur'an for forty days following the death of her mother-in-law. They then distributed food on the fortieth day to their friends and relatives, and prayed for the departed soul to rest in peace.

Those who are born have to leave this world. Thinking thus, she tried to comfort herself. She started to engage in her daily activities as before. It was time for Diwali. Fire crackers were burst non-stop. The temple authorities continued to honour them by providing them gingelly oil and shikakai powder on the day before Diwali. With the passage of time, Sultan Beevi Fathima gave birth to a baby boy. They named him as Jainulabdeen.

Grandpa Ibrahim Ambalam was delighted to hear about the birth of Ambalam Jainulabdeen Maraikayar. With the support of family elders, the children grew well. They were taught to recite the Holy Qur'an. They learnt the Tamil alphabets and were very disciplined. Along with Ibrahim Ambalam, Pakir Ambalam worked hard to expand their ancestral wealth and other properties. They plucked the coconuts and sold them. They plucked tamarind with the help of their workers and brought them home. The shells and seeds of the tamarind thus collected in their backyard were then removed.

They stored these in porcelain containers in their house. They distributed the rest to their relatives. People would come and ask them for these tamarinds. The children of the house - Seinambu and Jainulabdeen actively participated in all these activities. They would secretly consume these tamarinds with salt without the knowledge of their mother, and would later suffer from sore throat and fever. They then told about their little prank to their mother who had asked them for the reason. Sultan Beevi Fathima made arrow root decoction to cure them. Finally, their little tamarind prank came to an end.

Several days went by. Ibrahim Ambalam was searching for his brother's son after returning home from his evening prayer. When Pakir Ambalam approached him, Ibrahim Ambalam was lying in Avul Ambalam's huge cot. He held his nephew's hands tightly and said 'La ilaha illa Allah...' of the Kalima and passed away. His body finally found some rest. Even on his deathbed, he blessed his dear nephew. This was a huge loss to Pakir Ambalam for he had lost his dear mentor who carefully guided him in all the household as well as outside activities. The entire family mourned the death of Ibrahim Ambalam. However, Pakir was engaged in making all necessary arrangements. They seated their relatives and townsmen under a huge shamiana. A big sheep was cooked for the feast. After the Janazah prayer (This is the prayer for the departed soul that is done at the time of burial), when the Mayyit (both Janazah and Mayyit are terms used to represent the dead body) was taken, they served food to their friends and relatives from abroad and hometown. They also served food to the needy. The Holy Qur'an was recited for forty days and they prayed for the departed soul to rest in peace. Pakir Ambalam who was immersed in thoughts of his dead Chinaappa (younger brother of father), named his next born son as Ibrahim. After him, Mohaideen Seeni Avul, Sulaihamma and Ayishamma were born. Their family expanded.

It was time for the annual float festival of the Ramanathaswamy temple. As always, Pakir Ambalam constructed a boat with the help of his workers for the occasion. At the end of the ceremony, the temple authorities honoured Pakir Ambalam. He shared them with his dockyard workers.

Arrangements were made for railway transportation in Rameswaram. In order to construct the pathway, the railway department took some portions of Pakir Ambalam's ancestral land as well. He gave away the land unwillingly, as though he was separated from his own child. He pacified himself thinking that their land would serve the world in this way. Pakir Maraikayar and Sultan Beevi Fathima happily spent their time with their six children- Seinambu, Jainulabdeen, Ibrahim, Mohaideen Seeni Avul, Sulaiha, and Ayisha.

One afternoon, children rushed home carrying Mohaideen Seeni Avul who had gone to play outside. As he climbed the peepal tree, his legs slipped and he broke an arm. The doctor was summoned. He inspected the broken hand which was hanging loosely. As there were no other options, he had to amputate the hand. Pakir summoned many physicians (herbal doctors) to cure his son. The entire house smelt of herbal powders and oils. It had become a little clinic. Who can understand the will of God! Suffering from severe ailment and sickness, with his parents and siblings around him, Mohaideen Seeni Avul breathed his last. Pakir Ambalam suffered and cried uncontrollably looking at his sixteen-year old fair complexioned son who lay dead on his bed.

His relatives supported him by lifting him up and somehow made him perform the last rites for his son. Days and nights passed. However, Pakir Ambalam had become numb and had lost all his emotions and senses. Nothing and no one could pacify him. After his son's death, Pakir never left the house. He wasn't interested in anything anymore. He lost track of time. He wasn't bothered to look at sunrise and sunset. He stared at the horizon emptily. He didn't live long enough after that. Pakir Ambalam who had lost the power of speech also lost his physical strength after the death of his dear son. He too passed away. As a testimony to the popular saying *'Even an eyeless needle won't accompany you in your final journey'*, Pakir Ambalam who had expanded the ancestral property of the Ambalam family by growing sheep, cows named 'Kathija', coconut, palm and tamarind plantations left his mortal coils, leaving behind all his property to his family.

❑

Aerial Root - 3

"You both have so far heard the stories of our forefathers, Avul and Pakir, right? Now let me narrate the story of my father Jainulabdeen Maraikayar...", continued Maraikayar.

Since Jainulabdeen Ambalam had roamed around their ancestral properties on the plantations and the seashore with his father Pakir, he was able to handle all dealings related to these properties along with his brother Ibrahim when his father Pakir had become numb at the loss of his dear son Mohaideen Seeni Avul.

Maakkaan and Seenippeer came to their house one morning. These twin brothers were experts in sailing boats and fishing. Whenever the twins entered the sea for fishing, they would return only after their catch was full. They had come to their house to inform them that they were going fishing and had asked for some money for the purpose. Jainulabdeen Maraikayar gave them some money and asked them to send some fish to their house after their catch. He thought about the twin brothers as they were leaving. They were not just hard workers, but also gluttons. They even had special huge eating plates that were named after them as Maakkaan plate and Seenippeer plate. These plates were specially meant for them.

They were also extremely talented workers. Irrespective of the season, whether it was hot, stormy or rainy these two worked professionally. Akin to the popular saying, *'Those who ate well did well',* these two were always successful. Jainulabdeen Maraikayar shared his thoughts about the twin brothers Maakkaan and Seenippeer with his brother Ibrahim. People addressed 'Ambalam Jainulabdeen Maraikayar' as 'Jain Maraikayar.' Jain Maraikayar and Ibrahim Maraikayar would inspect their plantations and ask their labourers to collect coconuts and palm leaves. They frequented the seashore and inspected their fishing boats and sails. They also sold provision items in their shops. Everyday began with the morning prayer and would end with the 'Isha' prayer.

Their uncle Sahib Maraikayar assisted Jain Maraikayar and Ibrahim Maraikayar. He was the only son in Sultan Beevi Fathima's family. When the Britishers entered Rameswaram, they maintained cordial relations with him for all dealings of the British East India Company. He appointed a translator in order to correspond with them. Sahib Maraikayar had great interest in art and architecture. He constructed a beautiful white house using homeground mortar lime. In the entire neighbourhood, that was the first house to be built with stairs. Chairs with cushions and plush cots and beds decorated the house. Beautiful mirrors and lamps brought from England were used to beautify the house.

Sahib Maraikayar frequently invited the white men and their women for feasts in the house. At the huge kitchen situated in the backyard, his cooks prepared fried chicken coated with ghee and masala in huge iron pans. They also served rotis that were made using coconut milk. Sahib Maraikayar had two daughters - Kathija Nachiyar and Avulma Nachiyar. As he had no male progeny, he poured out all his affection to his sister's sons.

While he constructed his house, Sahib Maraikayar also constructed the Habil-Qabil Dargah using stones and mortar lime. One day, after finishing his morning prayer, Jain Maraikayar rushed to their coconut plantation for inspection. He asked the labourers to deliver the coconuts to their shop. He then asked his brother to take a few coconuts to their house and was returning back home via their Karaiyur plantation.

While he was approaching the square shed near the Enjiyadiyappa mosque, Abu Baker rushed towards him and said, "Your uncle has summoned you." Jain Maraikayar noticed that his uncle Sahib Maraikayar, his sister Alima's husband Vappa Sahib Maraikayar and others were seated in the square shed. Since Sahib Maraikayar knew that his nephew would come along that path to his house, he sent Abu Baker to fetch him. His uncle handed out a legal document and asked Jain Maraikayar to put the witness signature. As he was about to sign, his uncle told him, "First read the document thoroughly before signing."

He read the document carefully while standing in front of them. He refused to sign. Asking him to sit down, his uncle Sahib Maraikayar asked him, "Why are you refusing to sign?" That was a partition deed written after the death of one of their relatives. In the document, it was mentioned that 'Thaikka' which was a part of the mosque belonged to him. Since the relative had mentioned that a portion of the mosque was owned by him, Jain Maraikayar had refused to sign. He therefore asked them to bring him a revised document leaving out the 'Thaikka' section. He too accepted and left. Naina Muthammal was the elder sister of Seeni Naina Mohammad Maraikayar, Aliyar Maraikayar and Ibrahim Sahib Maraikayar. She was the mother of Vappa Sahib Maraikayar. Naina Muthammal who was tall and hefty was a brave lady. After finishing her household chores in the afternoon, she had the habit of visiting the Habil-Qabil Dargah with her lady relatives. She collected firewood over there. After that, they all bathed in the nearby well or a pond and returned back home carrying the firesticks. Whenever any men of the neighbourhood spotted these women relatives of the Ambalam family carrying firewood sticks, they made way for them.

Naina Muthammal could command many workers to do various jobs for her. However, she liked to do everything on her own. After her husband's death, she observed 'Iddah' and demanded from her sons that she too had the right to share her husband's property. As she was well-versed in the Holy Qur'an, she argued that as per the holy text, it has been specified that one-eighth of the share of the husband's property belonged to the wife after his death. (*Section-4; Chapter-4; Surah an-Nisa. In case you don't have any children, after your death, a quarter of your wealth belongs to your wife. However, if you have children, then after your death, one-eighth of your wealth should go to your wife.*) She eventually won in her argument. Everyone laughed at her saying, "Why does this old lady need any wealth?" However, Naina Muthammal was adamant in her stand.

Those who passed the judgement in Naina Muthamal's case agreed fully to her demand as they felt it to be just. Ultimately, Naina Muthammal's bold stance stood as a testimony to verses of the Holy Qur'an that gave the right to property for women. Days passed. Sultan Beevi Fathima was looking for a suitable proposal for her eldest daughter Seinambu Nachiyar. Her brother Sahib Maraikayar consulted their relatives and marriage was fixed between Qadar Pillai Maraikayar's son Mohammad Meera Sahib Maraikayar and Seinambu Nachiyar. With the approval of Qadar Pillai, the date for Seinambu-Mohammad Meera Sahib's marriage was fixed. The engagement was fixed for Friday evening. A big brass plate, a brass pitcher, brass cup for sandal paste and a gold finger ring were kept ready for the bridegroom. Fruits, sugar-candy, betel leaves, betel nuts, flowers, and turmeric tuber were kept ready on plates for the occasion.

Celebrations started from Friday morning onwards. Relatives from Pamban had come on bullock carts. The brass vessels in the house were neatly washed using tamarind. In the new plates, they kept betel leaves, turmeric tuber, jasmine flowers along with a thousand and one silver coins carefully wrapped in a piece of cloth. They covered the plate with a shining yellow cloth. In the other plates, they kept coconuts, fruits and sugar-candy. Sandal paste was kept in the cup. There were twenty-one items altogether. The menfolk sat down on mats in the bride's house. Uncle Sahib Maraikayar took the plate with the silver coins in both his hands. The other relatives took one plate each and headed to the bridegroom's house. They received a warm welcome in the bridegroom's house. They kept down the plates which bore the gifts. The engagement of Mohammad Meera Sahib Maraikayar and Seinambu happened smoothly in the presence of their friends and relatives.

Pesh Imam from the mosque prayed to God Almighty. Sahib Maraikayar handed over the plate to Qadar Pillai Maraikayar. He inserted the gold ring in the bridegroom's finger. Everyone in the room put some sugar in the bridegroom's mouth for auspiciousness. Sweets and savouries were served to all. After boiling the milk that was brought from the bride's family, they added some sugar-candies and distributed the sweet milk in tumblers to everyone. They then applied the sandal paste. They fixed the wedding date during the Shawwal month post Ramadan on the eleventh moon. Everyone left happily. They distributed the things given by the bride's family to their friends, workers and little children.

On the same day, during the early night hours, ladies from the bridegroom's family came to return the plates to the bride's family. They had filled up the plates with fruits, sweets and sugar. They received a warm welcome. Seinambu was standing coyly in a corner. She was made to sit in a comfortable chair. The eldest 'Sumangali' (married woman whose husband is still alive) in the bridegroom's family put some sugar in Seinambu Nachiyar's mouth as a mark of auspiciousness. They were served tea. While leaving, each of them were given the customary betel leaves, betel nuts and turmeric tubers. Days passed. It was the day before the first day of Ramadan. Bronze pan with lid, raw rice, jaggery, coconut, flowers, banana plantain, betel leaves and betel nuts were brought from the bridegroom's family to the bride's family. With the help of her brothers and sisters, Seinambu Nachiyar used the new pan to prepare cooked milk rice in the courtyard. They distributed some to the bridegroom's family as well.

On the evening of the first day of Ramadan, elders and youngsters prepared themselves for the occasion. The Ramadan days were spent by reciting Taraweeh, performing

Suhur, fasting during day time, and fast-breaking in the evening time. On the fifteenth day of Ramadan, they took a few items to the bridegroom's house as a part of the wedding paraphernalia. 101 coconuts, a sack of raw rice, a sack of jaggery, a measure of ghee, 101 eggs, greengram, and chana dal were packed in straw boxes and handed over to them.

They painted the house during Ramadan and made all necessary arrangements for the upcoming wedding ceremony. They ground fresh flour. They went to Madurai to purchase silk garments for the bride and groom. They personally invited all their relatives. Ramzan was declared after the sighting of the Shawwal moon. They visited the mosque, prayed and wished 'Eid Mubarak' to everyone. After consuming coconut rice and kari kurma, they performed six fasting rituals that had not been performed earlier. Everyone eagerly waited for Seinambu Nachiyar's wedding ceremony which was to happen after the 'six fasting rituals' were done.

Amidst the blessings and good wishes of their friends and relatives, the wedding ceremony of Seinambu and Meera Sahib happened in all pomp and glory. Seinambu bade goodbye to her dear mother, brothers and sisters, and left for Qadar Pillai Maraikayar's house as their bride. Many happy occasions came along. She had conceived which brought much joy to one and all. However, within the year, Seinambu Nachiyar died during childbirth. Her mother and siblings wailed uncontrollably. Over time, they began to heal slowly. Mohammad Muthu Meera Lebbai Maraikayar was Sahib Maraikayar's dad's younger brother Aliyar Maraikayar's son. He bought original pearls from the 'Silaabam' pearl seaport in Sri Lanka and sold them in India. He was a competent businessman.

His wife was Hasanachiyar. She belonged to the ancient 'Saanglibhava' house. Mohammad Asiyamma, Havva Ammal, Mohaideen Aliyar also known as Muthalib Maraikayar, and Ibrahim Sahib were the four children of the Mohammad Muthu Meera Lebbai Maraikayar-Hasanachiyar couple. He was very fond of his children. He made sure that his daughters too received a good education. A Christian lady named Kuzhanthaiyammal came to their house and taught them everyday. Asiyamma and Havvaamma became well-versed in Tamil.

Maraikayar maintained cordial relations with the Sethupathi kings who ruled over Ramanathapuram. Whenever the queens and the princesses of the palace visited Rameswaram to get a darshan of the Ramanathaswamy, they always visited the Maraikayar house in their palanquins. The wife of the palace Dewan as well as other ladies too accompanied them. They spent time with Hasanachiyar, Asiyamma and Havvamma. They sometimes left their maids with Asiyamma. These maidens who were in charge of decorating the queens and the princesses of the palace would try out various hairdos on Asiyamma and Havvamma.

They showed them how to do different hairstyles and other floral arrangements for the hairdo. They also trained them to stitch inner garments like blouses and petticoats. They taught them to prepare polis and laddus. They also learnt the food items prepared by the Maraikayar family members.

Days went by. Mohammad Muthu Meera Lebbai Maraikayar was a very tall man with a fair complexion. He lived happily with his wife and family. Suddenly he fell ill. He suffered from delirium and started blabbering. Forgetting their daily needs, his near and dear ones constantly monitored him. The family doctor Naagan was summoned. He rushed carrying his bag of medicines with him. In an earthen pot, he mixed the various powders sitting outside the house. As he was summoned inside, he checked the pulse of Mohammad Muthu Meera Lebbai Maraikayar. As their relatives eagerly waited for a positive response from doctor Naagan, he just said "The flower has now dried", and left. He threw away the earthen pot with the powder on the street. The pot broke into a hundred pieces. What could be said of the doctor who indicated subtly that his patient would die in such a compassionate manner!... Surrounded by his near and dear ones, Maraikayar died.

Asiyamma and her siblings were taken by shock at the loss of their beloved father. His elder and younger brothers cried uncontrollably. Even as they were slowly recovering from this huge loss, fate played with them in the form of cholera. The entire town was struck with cholera. There were heavy rains. Asiyamma and her siblings too suffered from cholera. Hasanachiyar lost her last son and Havvamma one after another and was heart-broken. Seeing his beloved sister's children die one after another, Sahib Maraikayar took Asiyamma and Muthalib who had survived with him to his house for treatment. As days passed the severity of cholera simmered and life returned back to normalcy.

Sahib Maraikayar decided to get his daughters married. In order to strengthen their family bonding, he decided to give his elder daughter Kathija Nachiyar's hand in marriage to his sister Sultan Beevi Fathima's eldest son Jain Maraikayar, and his younger daughter Avul Nachiyar's hand in marriage to his younger sister Havvamma's son Sayyid Ahmed. His sisters also agreed to this and wedding preparations were on. Everyone was busy with the arrangements. Sahib Maraikayar made beds out of teak wood for his daughters. Soft cotton mattresses were made for the cots. In the backyard, the ladies were busy preparing fresh flour. They made 'paniyarams' out of them. There were celebrations all around. Both daughters of Sahib Maraikayar got married to their designated spouses. They were then taken to the house of their husbands soon after marriage. Sahib Maraikayar sent various utilities to his children. The couples lived happily.

Kathija Nachiyar became pregnant. Her father Sahib Maraikayar felt very happy to hear the news of the arrival of his progeny.

Everyone took great care of Kathija Nachiyar. During the ninth month, her mother-in-law Sultan Beevi Fathima announced that she would bring 'Soola Paniyaram' to mark the occasion. As was customary, she summoned all her lady relatives, prepared Seepu paniyaram and Athirasam. She took these along with fresh banana plantains, flowers, betel leaves and betel nuts and left in the evening to see her daughter-in-law. Kathija Nachiyar wore her green silk wedding saree and was decked up in jewels and was made to sit on a comfortable chair. They made sweetened milk rice and distributed it to everyone. Having gone through a full cycle of pregnancy, Kathija Nachiyar who was decked up with flowers and jewellery beamed with joy. Time elapsed into seconds, minutes and hours. What happened next came as a shock to everyone!

Even before she could remove her silken garments, Kathija Nachiyar suffered from severe stomach pain. She started to sweat. The midwife was summoned urgently. In her futile attempts to deliver the dead baby inside, Kathija Nachiyar too lost her life. Sahib Maraikayar couldn't bear the loss of his dear daughter. Jain Maraikayar wept at the death of his dear wife. As days passed, many people approached Jain Maraikayar with suitable proposals. He did not agree to get remarried. He knew the mind of his uncle and father-in-law Sahib Maraikayar very well. He wanted him to get married to his brother Mohammad Muthu Meera Lebbai Maraikayar's daughter Asiyamma. Asiyamma had just then recovered from her cholera. She had lost a lot of weight and suffered from hair loss as a consequence of the disease. Her family did everything they could to bring her back to form. "When is she going to become a proper girl?" Everyone mocked her. However, wth the help of herbal medicines and vitamin supplements, Asiyamma turned into a beautiful maiden.

As days passed, Mohammad Muthu Meera Lebbai Maraikayar's father's younger brother Ibrahim Sahib Maraikayar died. His son Sultan Maraikayar and his elder brother's son Sahib Maraikayar installed lamp posts in three areas of the town as a mark of honour to him. These lamp posts were installed on the front, side and top corners of the mosque and lamps were lit throughout the night till the break of dawn. On the black stone in the posts were inscribed the words: *'In fond memory of Rameswaram (Late) Sriman M. M. Ibrahim Sahib Maraikayar Sahib Bahadur 1.7.1914.'*

Days went by. As per tradition, when a girl died young after her marriage, her husband would marry her younger sister. This was done to safeguard all properties that were given at the time of marriage as well as to take good care of her husband and children. (In Tamil, this was popularly known as 'Sondhaikku kattuthal' ('சோந்தைக்குக்

கட்டுதல்')). Therefore, Jain Maraikayar's sister Sulaihamma got married to Meera Sahib Maraikayar who had lost his wife. Jain Maraikayar arranged for the marriage of his brother Ibrahim with Alima Amma. His last daughter Ayishamma got married to Abdul Rahman Maraikayar from Pamban.

Jain Maraikayar who was waiting for nearly seven years got married to Asiyamma. Jain Maraikayar was very attached to his wife Asiyamma who was still a young maiden. Asiyamma, who was a devoted wife, would proudly say to others: "He always supports me even if I do any mischief. He adores me so much." Jain Maraikayar was such a calm and composed man. With the change of seasons and the passage of time, many children were born to the lovely couple. Jain Maraikayar's brother Ibrahim-Alima couple got a baby boy. They named him Samsuddin. His sister Ayishamma also gave birth to a baby boy. They had named him as Ahmed Jallaludin.

Jain Maraikayar's wife Asiyamma also became pregnant. However, the baby died inside her. She became pregnant a second time. She gave birth to a beautiful baby girl. They named her as 'Asim Zohara.'

Asiyamma was very fond of her paternal and maternal family members. She had great respect and reverence for her father's elder and younger brothers. Her father's younger brother, who had taken loan from the Devasthanam and was finding difficulty in repaying it approached Asiyamma for help. Without even consulting her mother and husband, she handed over her jewellery box containing 'Kaasu Maalai', 'Kandasaram', 'hand bracelet', 'shoulder bracelet', 'chain for the neck', 'long necklace chain', 'two-layered necklace' and so on weighing nearly five hundred sovereigns of gold to her uncle. Upon hearing this, Hasanachiyar was very upset as she had hand-picked each and every piece of jewellery for her beautiful daughter! Mother and daughter quarrelled with each other over the matter. However, Asiyamma didn't show even a trace of apprehension or concern. She gave no importance to material belongings even when she was young. She valued relationships over money and gained a special status among her peers. Ambalam Jainulabdeen Maraikayar, who knew the value of his wife, hardly bothered over the matter. He kept quiet. Next, Asiyamma gave birth to a baby boy. Everyone was drawn to this baby's handsome features.

Upon seeing this cute baby of her Jain Maraikayar uncle, Saluhamma who was Sultan Beevi Fathima's sister Havvamma's daughter rushed to her mom and said: "Umma, the colour of Jain Kaakaa's son is the same as the chain worn around its neck and hip, bangles, and its tiny little dress." Her mom asked her, "What are you saying, Saluha?''Saluhamma replied, "Yes, mom. Jain Kaakaa's son is of a golden hue and his accessories are all of a golden hue." Havvamma laughed at the description given by her daughter of her grandson. Jainulabdeen Ambalam named his son after his father-in-law as 'Mohammad Muthu Meera Lebbai Maraikayar.'

The baby grew and started to crawl and walk. He went to the kitchen and rolled all the utensils and other items over there and played joyfully. He poured all the ghee into his mouth and tasted it. He suffered from fever on account of drinking the ghee. The doctor was summoned. The medicines he gavc worked. The baby's fever subsided, however he was unable to walk. His parents panicked. All sorts of treatments failed to work. Finally, they decided to stay in the Habil-Qabil Dargah for forty days and packed all necessary materials in a bullock cart. They stayed over there with the baby.

It was customary for the Maraikayar family to stay in the Habil-Qabil Dargah for forty days and pray. Jain Maraikayar also followed this practice. They prayed to Habil and Qabil who were the sons of their first progenitor Adam for their baby's recovery. They performed the 'Duwah' (prayer done to fulfil a person's wish). They cried for their prayers to be heard. Since they had stayed in the Dargah for a particular reason, their relatives brought them rice, jaggery, fruits and other food items. After their afternoon lunch, the ladies of the house would come in covered bullock carts. They would be accompanied by a few male folk. They would come to the Dargah and enquire about the health of those who stayed there. They then did the Wudu ritual using the water from the Dargah well, and left after performing 'Asr' and 'Maghrib' prayers. If they came on a Thursday, they stayed overnight so that they could perform their Friday prayer rituals in the Dargah. They would wake up on Friday morning, perform their 'Fajr' prayer and return to their houses. On other days, they would return to their houses and perform their night time 'Isha' prayer.

At last, their prayers were heard. The boy's legs gained some strength. He started to walk. The little one took some water in a small pot from people who were taking water from the Dargah well. Looking at this, his mom felt thankful to God Almighty for restoring strength to her child. She felt that her boy fell ill only because she had named him after her father who had died at a very young age. Therefore, she started calling her boy as 'Chinna Maraikka' from that day onwards. Her mom Hasanachiyar too, who was so far unable to address the child using her husband's name, felt happy about this. Everyone started to call the young one as 'Chinna Maraikka.' Asiyamma was very fond of the brilliant child. Once again, Asiyamma became pregnant. Her mom Hasanachiyar took good care of her. After ten months, she gave birth to a beautiful girl child. They named her as 'Hajara.'

Chinna Maraikka played happily with his elder sister Asim Zohara and younger sister Hajara. He would share all his toys with his young sister Hajara who had curly hair and a fair complexion. He would fondly address her as 'Hajaramma.' The effect of World War I was felt even in Rameswaram which was in the farthest corner of India. People talked about war news all the time. As India was a British colony, many Indians had to fight for the British and lost their lives.

During World War I, after Turkey lost, Mustafa Kamal Badshah overthrew the reign of the earlier Sultan. He became the founding father of the Republic of Turkey and was therefore addressed as 'Ata Turk' which means 'Turkey's father' by people all over the world.

Asiyamma, who became pregnant during this time, gave birth to a baby boy. Since Jain Maraikayar was greatly drawn towards the achievements of 'Mustafa Kamal Badshah', he named his son after him as Mustafa Kamal. With their two sons and two daughters, Asiyamma and Jain Maraikayar lived a peaceful life. They lost their beautiful girl Hajara to measles. Everyone mourned the little one's death.

Jain Maraikayar's brother Ibrahim Maraikayar and his wife Alima Ammal had children named Sultan Beevi Fathima and Ahmed Meera Lebbai after Samsuddin. Jain Maraikayar regarded his brother's children as his own. He was fond of his brother Ibrahim Maraikayar. They shaved the heads of all the boy children of the family. The children were made to wear caps, dhotis and pyjamas and were sent to the mosque to learn and recite the Holy Qur'an. They were sent to school and started learning the alphabets 'A', 'Aa'...The Tamil teacher 'Muthu Pillai' had great regards and respect for the Maraikayar family. He addressed the Maraikayar children as 'Master' and taught them Tamil.

The Maraikayar brothers took their children to their plantations and other properties. The children played happily in the sand on the ground. The children accompanied the elders to the seashore and their shops as well. Mohammad Ibrahim Maraikayar was very fond of his brother. He had great respect for him. He loved his brother's son 'Chinna Maraikka' very much. While he went to purchase banana plantains for all the children, he always bought regular bananas for the other children. However, since Chinna Maraikka would spit it out, he bought special mountain bananas for him. Asiyamma did not like to send her son Chinna Maraikka outside with anyone. The first reason was because he was very handsome. The second reason was his naughty pranks. However, Mohammad Ibrahim Maraikayar always took Chinna Maraikka with him. He was very fond of his dear brother's son. There was no end to Chinna Maraikka's pranks. While their doctor's car passed by their shop, he rolled coconuts in front of the car. The car lost balance. However, since the doctor was a skilled driver, he managed to reposition it back to safety. As he was looking outside to see who the culprit was, he saw Chinna Maraikka.

Since he was fond of the Maraikayar brothers, he did not report the incident to them. When this news reached Jain Maraikayar, he searched for his son to give him some sound advice. However, Ibrahim Maraikayar hid his brother's son out of sight till the matter cooled down.

Just like Mohammad Ibrahim Maraikayar, his maternal uncle Muthalib Maraikayar too was very fond of Chinna Maraikka. Enjoying the naughty pranks of the little one, he taught him how to be brave and bold. Muthalib Maraikayar was the brother of Jain Maraikayar's wife Asiyamma. He was hefty and stout. He maintained their properties and poured out his affection towards his sister, her husband and their children.

The children were very close to their maternal grandmother Hasanachiyar and maternal uncle Muthalib Maraikayar. Hasanachiyar, who was Jain Maraikayar's mother-in-law, was also Mohammad Maraikayar's aunt's daughter. Mohammad Maraikayar, who was Thummuni Maraikayar's grandson and Seenippeer Maraikayar's son was affectionate towards his aunt's daughter Hasanachiyar and her daughter Asiyamma. Asiyamma addressed him as 'Chacha' since he was like her dad's brother to her. Mohammad Maraikayr's first wife had two children - Mohaideen Seeni Avul and Abdul Zafar. Since his wife had died after giving birth to his two sons, he got married to her sister later. She lived for a very short span of time, leaving no children behind.

He then got married a third time since he needed some support in taking care of his children. He got a son named 'Abdul Jalal' from her. She died soon after giving birth to this child and Mohammed Maraikayar once again became lonely. Asiyamma felt very sad that her Chacha and her brothers had to suffer without the care and nurturing support of women at home. Many people approached with suitable proposals. Mohammad Maraikayar wouldn't budge. His aunt's daughter Hasanachiyar, and her daughter Asiyamma insisted upon his marriage. People from Pamban approached them with a marriage proposal for Mohaideen Peeramma. Her Chacha Mohammad Maraikayar asked Asiyamma to go visit the bride. As soon as she saw Peerma, Asiyamma felt that she was the right bride for her Chacha's family. She convinced her Chacha accordingly. The marriage was fixed. The wedding day was fast approaching.

Asiyamma was wearing a dull-coloured saree. Her Chacha Mohammed Maraikayar asked her to wear something bright for the occasion. Despite the hectic marriage preparations, he said this to Asiyamma as she was like his own daughter to him. Asiyamma wore a beautiful pink coloured saree and left in a bullock cart to attend her Chacha's wedding. Peerammal came to live in Thoona Cheena's house as their bride. She gave birth to a baby girl the next year. They named her as 'Ahmed Kaniyamma.' This girl later became the wife of Asiyamma's eldest son Chinna Maraikka. Asiyamma, who had stayed in her maternal house, gave birth to a baby boy. Since Jain Maraikayar maintained cordial relations with the Mandapam Maraikayar family, he named his son after Kasim Mohammed Maraikayar who was living a luxurious life at the time.

After Ramzan and Bakrid festivities, it was now time for Diwali and Pongal. They received gingelly oil, shikakai powder, pots for Pongal, vegetables, fruits, coconuts and other items from the temple as always. Jain Maraikayar kept everything in straw boxes and handed them over to his brother Ibrahim Maraikayar. One day, Chinna Maraikka was suffering from severe neck pain. They did their best to treat him. However, no medication worked. They then summoned the local herbal physician Aandimagan. He said that they had to apply a special kind of oil for treating Chinna Maraikka.

Aandimagan had suggested making oil from an ant. (This ant was slightly bigger than the ants that bite. This is a rare variety of ant that usually grows in the bark of Jamun trees.) They arranged for it. Since the labourers had to fetch those eggs while bearing the pain of the ant bites, they asked for a huge sum of money. After they agreed, they brought half a measure of those eggs. These eggs were slightly bigger than the lizard eggs and were white in colour. Aandimagan collected different herbal leaves, neem oil and other items. He left everything at the backyard and left for the day. He said that he would visit them the next day to prepare the necessary concoction for treatment.

Asiyamma's father's younger brother Mohammed Maraikayar heard of the news of his grandson's neck pain and had bought R.S. Pathi pain balm from Madurai for treatment. He had heard from the shopkeeper in Madurai that it could cure all sorts of pains. As soon as he came back, he handed over the bottle to his daughter Asiyamma. The medicine was applied on the boy's neck.

The next morning Chinna Maraikka got completely cured. It was because of the R.S. Pathi pain balm. (Till this day, R.S. Pathi pain balm appears on the monthly provision list of the Maraikayar family. The credit for this should go to Mohammed Maraikayar for introducing it, and to his future son-in-law Chinna Maraikka for using it. This is also shipped to various places like Chennai, Bangalore, Mangalore, Delhi, Abu Dhabi, Muscat, and Qatar where the younger generation of the Maraikayar family work presently.) The whole family felt relieved.

Aandimagan came to prepare the concoction the following day. Mohammed Maraikayar who had great respect for Aandimagan showed him the medication that had cured his grandson. Aandimagan was glad that Chinna Maraikka felt better now and left with the payment received from the Maraikayar brothers. Chinna Maraikka roamed around their family plantations, other properties and seashore after leaving school. His friend was Alauddin whom Chinna Maraikka and his brothers addressed as 'uncle' since he was related through 'Avvakkkarappa.'

Chinna Maraikka and Alauddin were standing outside the pot shop. Different types of pots and pans were arranged over there. Alauddin was very excited that day. He told Chinna Maraikka, "Hey son-in-law (that's how he addressed him normally)! How would it be if we tapped these pots with sticks?" to which Chinna Maraikka replied, "Like this…" He tapped one pot and one fell over the other and all pots and pans crumbled to pieces soon after. The shop owner got upset. Jain Maraikayar, upon hearing this news, rushed to the shop with a stick to hit his son. Chinna Maraikka's maternal uncle Muthalib Maraikayar hid him out of sight in his house for a while. He then gave some money as compensation for the shopkeeper's loss.

Chinna Maraikka would visit his house to see his mom and elder sister Asim Zohara while his father was away. His childhood was filled with such pranks and playfulness. The little boys were growing big now. In the following rainy season, one of their pregnant cows that had gone to graze was lost. They got tired of instructing the cow-catchers about it. Mohammed Ibrahim Maraikayar, who suffered from a mild headache, became sick suddenly. The fever was followed by delirium. Ibrahim Maraikayar, who always adhered to his religious practices such as reciting the Holy Qur'an and praying, realised that he was now on his deathbed.

He sent for his 'kaakka' and asked Allah to forgive all his sins that he might have committed in his lifetime.

He also told his elder brother of the dream he had had the previous night. He had dreamt that the pregnant cow that they had lost, had now delivered a calf and was stationed at a place. The cow-catchers were summoned immediately. The cow and the calf were standing at the exact spot suggested by Ibrahim Ambalam. They fetched the cow and the calf and tied them in the backyard of their house. Even at the time of his death, Ibrahim Maraikayar had restored one of their family's belongings. He died peacefully. Jain Maraikayar was heart-broken at the loss of his dear brother. After completing the burial rituals, he sat down in the wooden chair. He was lost in thoughts. He never got up from that chair for forty days. Since Jain Maraikayar forgot about his house and other properties after the death of his beloved brother, he stopped instructing his workers. As a result of this, the coconuts in their plantation fell one after another without getting plucked. Seemed like even the trees in their plantations missed Ibrahim Maraikayar!

The maintainers of their plantations visited their house frequently and reminded him. However, Jain Maraikayar, who was lost in thoughts of his brother, hardly bothered to instruct them. They collected the coconuts and piled them up in the house's backyard. His children felt sorry for their father. Chinna Maraikka and Samsuddin now took charge of their properties. Everyday, they would leave from their house after performing the 'Fajr' prayer and would be back home right on time for the 'Dhuhr' prayer. Since Chinna Maraikka knew all about their plantations, he wasn't finding any difficulty in handling them. However, Samsuddin, who was used to handling their shops in town, wasn't comfortable dealing with the plantations. He asked Chinna Maraikka to take care of them and left to deal with the shops.

After his younger brother's death, a few cruel people decided to play with the feelings of the Maraikayar family members. Soon after Ibrahim Maraikayar's death, a few relatives approached his wife Alima Ammal, and told her, "Alimamma, if you agree, we will fight for the property rights for you and your children, and we can secure half the property." They wanted to turn her against Jain Maraikayar. However, that noble lady simply said, "Let all property go to Jain Maraikayar itself." She never left her husband's house, nor did she show any aversion or hatred towards his family members. When Jain Maraikayar heard of this, he felt thankful to Alima Ammal for placing all her trust in him.

Slowly he started to recover from the shock of his brother's death. He took great care of his children as well as his brother's children. He regarded all of them equally. He now joined hands with the children to run the textile industry which he had started with his brother. He also took care of their other properties well. The elder sister and brother had a difference of opinion and Asiyamma left for her husband's house along with her children. Since their house was no longer sufficient for their growing family, Jain Maraikayar constructed a house in the piece of land opposite to their place. This land had been purchased by him and his brother Ibrahim. He decided to stay in the new house with his wife and children. At this time, Jain Maraikayar was suffering from an abscess on his tongue. They took him to the government hospital for treatment. After checking him thoroughly, the doctor said, "I will give a written statement as my medical advice. You please take him to Madurai hospital for further treatment. He needs three injections. They can do that over there based on the availability of the medicine. Otherwise, the cost of one injection is three thousand rupees. You might have to get it yourself and ask them to inject him." Since Jain Maraikayar was finding it difficult to eat and sleep peacefully, they decided to take him to Madurai for treatment. Nine thousand rupees was a huge amount of money in those days. Even then, no one objected. They all unanimously decided to go to Madurai.

His mother Sultan Beevi Fathima, who was looking at all this, said, "You cannot take my son to Madurai. What will happen if something bad happens to him over there? Shouldn't we at least be able to perform the Mayyith rituals?." She cried uncontrollably. She then suggested, "Why not show him to Muthukaruppan's son Murugan for treatment?" Jain Maraikayar, who knew his mother's sharp mind, decided to cancel his Madurai trip. Murugan was summoned.

After inspecting him thoroughly, Murugan said, "We have to give him some vapour treatment", and got into action. The flakes of dried drumstick trees were collected. In the morning, these were heated in a new earthen pot. When they started heating up, he put the medicinal powder that he had brought with him. He then covered it with a blanket and asked Jain Maraikayar to bring out his tongue so that the hot vapour touched it. Jain Maraikayar was already suffering from tongue abscess. Now after this vapour treatment, he couldn't even drink water. The doctor applied boiled, cooled goat's milk on his tongue with a cotton ball. By the Grace of God, within the next three days, the abscess dried and fell out. Within the next few days, Jain Maraikayar started to consume liquid and solid foods.

His mother, wife, sisters, children, brother's children, friends and relatives thanked God for His mercy. After he had fully recovered, Jain Maraikayar decided to shift to the new roof house which he was constructing.

Both Jain Maraikayar and Ibrahim Maraikayar were very fond of their sister Ayishamma who lived with her husband in Pamban. Even when she was a child, they wouldn't let her roam barefeet. They bought her special boots to walk around. Ayishamma, who got married in all pomp and glory, returned with her children to her mother's house one day crying vehemently. She had had a fight with her mother-in-law. Her brother and mother tried to convince and pacify her. However, she said she would never go back to Pamban again and stayed with them.

In the meantime, brother Muthalib Maraikayar had resolved his quarrel with sister Asiyamma and so Asiyamma returned back to her mother's house. Jain Maraikayar wanted to do something for his dear sister Ayishamma. Asiyamma suggested something. She asked her husband to make Ayishamma settle down in the house built for her. On an auspicious day, Ayishamma settled down in the new house along with her husband and children. Incidentally, Kadar Pillai's house was right next to Ayishamma's house. Ayishamma's children who were very fond of their Periyamma (aunt), Kadar Pilla's daughter-in-law Sulaihamma, felt jubilant. The elders in the family wanted Ayishamma's two daughters to get married to their Chinna Kaakka's son Samsuddin and Periya Kaakaa's son Chinna Maraikka.

Who could know about the intentions of Allah! From Ayishamma's eldest son Ahmed Jallaluddin to her youngest son Noordin, all of her children played in their Ummamma's and Periyamma's houses. They became children of Rameswaram. Samsuddin Maraikayar would offer his support to his aunt's children as they had come away from their hometown Pamban. He took them everywhere and showed them all the places. Samsuddin was very close to Ahmed Jallaluddin and became his good friend.

Jain Maraikayar wanted to construct a house for himself once again. He started to construct it by laying the foundation in their ancestral land which was a piece of land that belonged to Avul Ambalam's brother Ibrahim Ambalam. He wanted to build a house to stay in. At that time, neither did he know that the first-born in this house was about to become a great legend nor did he know that this house was going to become famous! God alone knows everything! One day, Honourable Abdul Rahman Maraikayar had come to visit them. (Since he had good conduct, the Britishers gave him the title 'Honourable' to mark his noble character.) Jain Maraikayar's mom Sultan Beevi Fathima was his aunt's daughter. He had come there to invite for his son Abdul Salam's wedding. Since the bride belonged to 'Maraikayar Pattinam' the wedding location was fixed there.

The previous day, when he had come from Pamban to Rameswaram, he had said, "Machi (in case the daughters of someone's uncles or aunts were elder to them, people addressed them as 'Machi'. It is also customary to address the elder brother's wife and sister-in-law as 'Machi'), without you, I won't leave", and stayed in their house. In those days, the ladies wouldn't board the train alone. Out of courtesy, Jain Maraikayar sent his mother Sultan Beevi Fathima along with his son, brother's son, his daughter and brother's daughter to attend the function.

Abdul Rahman Maraikayar accompanied his Machi and grandchildren from Rameswaram, got down at Mandapam Camp and boarded the bullock cart that was stationed there to Maraikayar Pattinam where the wedding was about to happen. The children enjoyed the train and the bullock cart journey very much. Chinna Maraikka and Samsuddin went around the place with their peers. Asim Zohara and Thangamma sat down quietly with their Vappumma (Grandma-father's mom) throughout the function. Abdul Rahman Maraikayar honoured his Machi throughout the ceremony by giving her the first rights to all the events. The marriage happened smoothly by God's grace. Chinna Maraikka's Ummamma (mom's mom) Hasanachiyar had many relatives in Maraikayar Pattinam. When they heard that their grandchildren had accompanied grandma Sultan Beevi Fathima, they all went to see them. O.M. Okasu Maraikayar and Periyamma Nachiyar's family members took them to their house.

It was summer after the monsoon. Ayishamma's daughter Ummuhalima who was fondly called as Ummalima by one and all. She was a very weak girl. Afflicted by an incurable ailment, she passed away. The children and the elders were upset over her loss. As days went by, the bell rings from Rameswaram temple were heard. It was customary for the bells to be rung during the daily pooja rituals at the temple. The children were curious to know the reason. So they asked the family elders. Asiyamma, who was fond of narrating historic tales, answered them based on what she had heard from others. The children eagerly listened to her. People from all corners of India come to Rameswaram to pray to their God. For those people who took the 'Kasi Yatra' pilgrimage, Rameswaram was the final destination. The bells were rung to indicate that people with Ganga water in their hands had come to Rameswaram to bathe in the holy waters there.

From Ramanathapuram to Rameswaram, the palace workers would ring the bells to announce that people with Ganga water are approaching. Also, when the Sethupati rulers from Ramanathapuram came to have a darshan of the God in the temple, they rang the bell for the people to make way for them. Nowadays, after roads have been properly laid, it has become customary for temple bells to be rung during the everyday pooja rituals. The children who were intently listening to Asiyamma understood that ringing of the bell symbolised the time for prayer.

Ayishamma's son Noordeen died of an ailment. The elders and youngsters of the house felt miserable over the loss. In order to distract them from their misery, Asiyamma would narrate different stories to them. She brought cooked rice with fish curry in a huge plate. She then made the children sit around her. She would make huge balls of rice and curry and give it to them in their hands and then she would start her narration. That day, the story was about the Rameswaram temple bell. The bell announced that it was 1 PM.

Asiyamma asked them, "Do you know what the time is now?..." "1 PM" they said after listening to the ring of the bell. "Yes, you are correct", she said and continued, "From where is this bell being rung?" to which they replied, "From the temple." "In 1902, a foreigner Bahambar Verine gave a metallic bell which was 3 feet tall and 3 feet wide, weighing nearly 600 Kgs to the temple. If this bell is rung, it echoes beyond our town so that people living outside too would be able to listen to it. The local fishermen as well as people living in Rameswaram, Pamban, Mandapam and Talaimannar calculate the time only by listening to the sound of this bell", explained Asiyamma in detail. The children listened to her story eagerly and had finished eating by then.

"Is Ambalam there?" Someone called from outside. The children looked to see who was calling. It was Jain Maraikayar's friend Ramanatha Sastrigal. Since the children knew him already, they started narrating the tale of the temple bell that they had heard. After listening to them earnestly, he said, "Every morning, it is time for 'Thiruvananthal pooja' at 6 AM, 'Vila' pooja at 7 AM, 'Kaala Shanti' pooja at 10 AM. Then at 12 noon, during 'Artha Jama pooja', the bell will be rung continuously for ten minutes. At night, the bell will be rung for every hour starting from 9 PM. This is done so that people can identify the correct time even without looking at the clock." He added some extra information so that the children understood clearly.

Ayishamma then gave birth to a baby boy. They named him 'Noordeen' after her son Noordeen who had passed away.

The house that Ambalam Jainulabdeen Maraikayar was building for over eleven years had reached almost completion. He couldn't allot enough time to his family during this time. Asiyamma's mother Hasanachiyar helped a lot with the construction of this house for her daughter. After her husband Mohammed Muthu Meera Lebbai Maraikayar's death, many of their neighbours excluding a few, tried to snatch away her property. Therefore, whatever he had earned for his family members disappeared soon after his death. His daughter Asiyamma too gave away her jewellery and her mom's jewellery to everyone out of benevolence. Jain Maraikayar also did not want to take anything from the common property for constructing his house. He only used the money he had earned all by himself for constructing the house. Hasanachiyar, therefore sold her utensils and gave the money for the construction of her daughter's house. Her financial support also helped in completing the construction.

An auspicious day was fixed for shifting to the new house. The house was south-facing, with two pials at the front, two floors, and a backyard. In the first level, thatched roof was laid on all four sides surrounding the central hall made out of bricks that had a central courtyard. This layout is known as 'four-laned house' since there were four lanes laid around the central hall. In the back side, there was a huge room. Since Jain Maraikayar wanted his brother's daughter to get married at the same time as his daughter, he built one more room opposite this huge room. Since there wasn't enough space to erect a wall of bricks, he had used wooden planks to erect wooden walls instead. There were two pials at the back, opposite to which was a huge kitchen with thatched roof. At the extreme back end was a lavatory meant for ladies. The piece of land that was to the west of the well was given to Sultan Beevi Fathima's sister Havvamma's husband Mustafa Sahib at the time of their wedding. Since the houses of the two sisters were near one another, the usage of Pakir Ambalam's well was equally shared among the sisters.

Therefore, in order to distinguish their portion of the well, Jain Maraikayar had installed a layer made of straws, stones, and a fence at the centre of the well. He then arranged for a design to draw water from the well. (This he did by planting two huge trees near one another. These were 10-15 feet away from the well and a stick was attached to this mechanism to which a rope was then attached to draw water from the well. This rope was made of soft materials so that it wouldn't hurt one's hands while drawing out the water. A bucket was tied to the rope to draw water.) At the backyard were cow sheds, places to assemble hay and straw, and a thatched roof compartment meant for hot water bath. The house had been neatly plastered and the windows painted and decorated beautifully and kept ready for the house-warming ceremony. On an auspicious day, they woke up before 4 AM, and after performing the Tahajjud Namaz, they got ready. Accompanied by his mother, wife, mother-in-law, brother-in-law, sisters, brother's wife, brother's children, sister's children, and other relatives, with the Holy Qur'an in his hand, Jain Maraikayar chanted 'Bismillah' and settled down in his new house. His wife carried her treasure chest, salt, milk and chanting prayers, she entered keeping her right foot first inside the house.

Jain Maraikayar invited Avvakkar to come to the front to recite a few verses of prayer. This Avvakkar was none other than Abu Baker, who came to be known as 'Avvakkaarappa' by one and all. He was regarded as a member of their own family.

Kind-hearted Abu Baker Ravuthar started his prayer with 'Allahu Akbar' and did the 'Duwah' (prayer) by opening both his palms. Hasanachiyar had bought new silk saree, silk dhoti, dresses for children, a new bronze pot with a lid, huge spoons meant for cooking, a sack of raw rice, coconut, jaggery, fruits, betel leaves, betel nuts among other items and spread them all out in the hall for her daughter's family. Following her, their relatives gifted them with copper water-pot, metallic pots, huge vessels, pitchers and so on based on their convenience. The Maraikayar family invited them with warm hearts and made them sit on decorated mats.

Asiyamma kept salt, milk and other kitchen items inside the kitchen of their brand-new house which was going to become the residence of several generations of the Maraikayar family members. "Ya Allah", she prayed to Allah for peace and harmony in the house and started boiling the milk in the huge pan that was gifted to her by her mother. After adding sugar, the milk was distributed to the people present there. As they hear the call for the 'Fajr' prayer, Jain Maraikayar left from his new house to the mosque to pray along with his relatives.

The ladies of the house did the 'Wudu' ritual and prayed. They offered tea to the men who had returned home after praying. Then, in the huge hall, they prepared sweetened milk rice and distributed it to the people gathered there. They also prepared idiyappam for breakfast. After breakfast, they spread out mats at the hall and recited the 'Mawlid.' Alimsa and Modhinar recited the prayer along with music to honour Prophet Muhammad (Peace Be Upon Him). Sweetened milk rice kept in large porcelain plates known as 'Sahan', equal measures of sugar-candy, dates, fruits, pomegranate seeds, cut guava and other fruit varieties along with the smell of fresh sandal paste and agarbatti that decorated the house filled the entire house with good fragrance.

After Alimsa had finished, Jain Maraikayar prayed (Duwah) for his family. The sweetened milk rice was then distributed to their relatives. They gave some to Miskin who was standing outside their house and had called out to them. They then served food on banana leaves to the men and the children who had returned from the 'Dhuhr' prayer. Their relatives returned to their respective houses after blessing the Maraikayar family. The workers from the seashore, plantations, cleaners, gardeners, washermen, barber and others came to their house, and after eating, they took some food to their houses. By the time the ladies of the house and other workers had eaten, it was time for 'Asr' prayer. The children played in their new house. In the evening, they lit the lamp to welcome their first night in the new house.

Time went by and seasons changed. Many pilgrims had come to Rameswaram from north India and other parts of India for the Shivaratri celebration. After the early morning fourth Jama pooja, Spadigalinga pooja and special abhishekam and aradhana (Abhishekam is a religious ritual in which a devotee pours a liquid offering to the linga/ murthi. Aradhana is the recitation of special prayers to invoke the deity) were done. After this, the lord and his consort were taken on a procession. Many devotees pulled the chariot. After travelling on all four sides, the ratha (Chariot) halted. Based on the timings of the Shivaratri, the devotees poured Ganga water and did the abhishekam to Ramanathaswamy. In the evening, Swamy and Ambal did their procession along all four sides on golden horse chariots. After the usual rituals, the Shivaratri celebration came to an end. People from all parts of India were assembled to witness this major celebration.

One morning, Asiyamma was feeling a bit uneasy. Her mother Hasanachiyar, upon seeing her daughter's condition, informed Asiyamma's mother-in-law Sultan Beevi Fathima, "I think your daughter-in-law is about to give birth", to which she replied, "Hasanachi, finish all work as soon as possible. We need to summon the midwife to deliver the baby." She then called out to her son Jain Maraikayar and informed him of the news. Jain Maraikayar had had many children previously with his wife. However, he was perplexed to look at her while she was going through labour pain. This is going to be the first child to be born in their new house. He looked at his wife reassuringly and prayed to God Almighty.

Hasanachiyar kept the house ready for the newborn. She gave a decoction prepared by putting cumin seeds in hot water to her daughter. She then kept the neatly washed sarees and white dhotis that would come of help during labour time. In between all this, she did the Wudu ritual and did Duwah for a safe delivery. When her son asked her, "What's for dinner?" She replied "Rava Upma '', and served it to her son-in-law, her daughter's mother-in-law, granddaughter and grandsons. She also made her daughter eat a few spoons of it.

Meanwhile the midwife had arrived. She asked, "Have you given her the jeera water decoction?" to which

Hasanachiyar replied, "Yes, I gave it to her a while ago." She then served some tiffin to the lady. Hearing the news, their lady relatives arrived there. Asiyamma who was lying in the huge room welcomed all of them warmly. Out of labour pain, she was screaming, 'Ya Allah' in between her pangs.

The first child to be born in that huge room at the back side of their house. No one would have thought that this child was going to become a world-famous scientist or as a President of India one day! They all eagerly awaited the arrival of the baby. At the break of dawn, when it was time for the 'Fajr' prayer, the baby's first screams were heard. The men who were seated outside the house thanked God for His mercy. The other children of the house woke up and rushed in to see their little brother. This infant with its tiny little hands and legs and with a huge tuft of hair greatly captivated the young children.

God alone knew that this little baby born on October 15, 1931, was going to create history and that his name would be written in golden letters. Asiyamma was very fond of this child. Out of fascination towards freedom fighter 'Abul Kalam Azad', they named this baby as 'Abdul Kalam.' With its mother's affection, the baby grew with a sharp mind. They wanted to complete the 'Sunnath' ritual for all the male children.

They performed the Sunnath for all of them starting from the eldest Samsuddin till the new born Abdul Kalam.

His mom Asiyamma was very much worried about Abdul Kalam as he was just an infant. She had to agree to her husband's command in the end. This was going to be the first function to be celebrated in their new house. Everyone was feeling happy. They soaked raw rice in water and with the help of workers ground them in mortars and prepared the rice flour. Sultan Beevi Fathima and Hasanachiyar prepared the idiyappam powder. They went and invited their relatives in Pamban, Mandapam, Vedalai and Maraikayar Pattinam. They installed a huge shamiana and banana trees at the front of the house to mark the occasion. They also installed a shamiana in the backyard. They prepared rice in huge quantities and served all their guests. Their workers rushed to their house after hearing the news about the ceremony.

Other than his sons and his brother's sons, Jain Maraikayar had also arranged for the 'Sunnath' ceremony for three poor children in their neighbourhood. He bought clothes from Madurai for all of them. All their relatives had arrived right in time for the function. In the morning, they had arranged for the hair cutting ceremony. A barber from Pamban was summoned to perform the 'Sunnath.' Starting from the eldest, all their relatives presented dupattas for the occasion. The names of each of them were announced, and a huge pile of colourful dupattas were collected.

Out of nearly 300 dupattas that were accumulated, they presented a few to the local doctors. The rest were shared between the barber and the washerman of the house. They were all happy to receive them from their boss's family. The children were made to sit in a line and the barber shaved their faces. They were then made to take their bath. After wearing their new clothes, they were all sent to their grandmother. Sultan Beevi Fathima and Hasanachiyar blessed them and did Duwah for their well-being. After everyone ate their lunch, garlands were put around the children's neck. Drums were struck and the children were made to sit on horsebacks and were taken on a procession. The relatives whose houses were along the way garlanded and gave milk to these Sunnath boys going on a procession.

The relatives who had accompanied the boys in the procession handed over handfuls of betel nuts to those who garlanded the boys. The procession stopped at the mosque. They then recited the Fathiha, did the Duwah at the mosque and returned back home in a procession. At home, the boys were made to sit on a mortar and the barber did the 'Sunnath' procedure for all of them. The boys were then made to lie down in the hall. The boys who came from other houses for Sunnath returned back to their respective homes with their family members. Jain Maraikayar helped their families for seven days. They were provided with meals three times every day. Whenever the barber came to look at the Maraikayar boys, he sent him to the houses of the poor boys' family as well for inspection.

Abdul Kalam's mother Asiyamma kept him on her lap and took care of him. On the seventh day, the children took a head bath in hot water. They prepared sweetened milk rice and distributed them in huge quantities to their relatives to announce that the seventh day ceremony had been performed. They then gave the barber dhoti, towel, raw rice, coconut, and banana along with the money for his services. As days went by, Abdul Kalam too joined others and went to Madrasa to learn the Holy Qur'an. He was sent to the local school for formal education. With the little boy in one hand and a hurricane lamp in his other hand, Jain Maraikayar would leave everyday morning at 4 AM to drop him to the local school.

This school was also known as 'Samiyar school.' The person in-charge of this school would ask the children to come to school after bathing everyday. Therefore, Asiyamma would make Abdul Kalam bathe everyday early in the morning. Next Abdul Kalam went to the Government Primary School for elementary education.

Isn't it true that friendship and enmity come one after the other in life! Someone in the mosque created a rift among the relatives by invoking a superiority complex. On account of this, the relationship between the Jain Maraikayar family and Mohammad Maraikayar family was cut off. One day, Mohammad Maraikayar had come to the house opposite to Jain Maraikayar to collect the house rent. With him was his daughter Ahmed Kaniyamma with her little brother on her hips. He had asked the children to wait outside while he collected the rent. Ahmed Kaniyamma was about to sit on the pedestal outside the Jain Maraikayar house. "Hey! You can't sit here. My Periyappa would get angry. Run away", said Jain Maraikayar's younger brother's son Mahmud Abu Baker. Ahmed Kaniyamma left the place with her little brother.

Looking at his daughter, Mohammad Maraikayar asked, "What is the matter?" "Nothing actually", she replied. "Did he ask you not to sit outside their house?" he asked mockingly and left with his children. As he was going back, he looked at his daughter and blessed her for her kind heart. Neither he nor his daughter knew at the time that Ahmed Kaniyamma would marry Chinna Maraikka one day and would take all responsibility in handling the Maraikayar family matters! Who can understand the divine will of God Almighty!

Since the two families were adrift, most of the functions happened without the presence of many relatives. When Ahmed Kaniyamma attained puberty, they had arranged for a big feast and had invited everyone for the grand ceremony. One of their women relatives was upset that Jain Maraikayar's family members had not been invited. She asked Mohammed Maraikayar, "Listen to me. You also have a son and a daughter and he too has a son and a daughter. If you both quarrel amongst yourselves, then how can you both become relatives in future?" Mohammed Maraikayar replied, "Quarrels are quarrels and relationships are relationships." As he had great interest in epics, he would sit with his peers and sing verses from Kamba Ramayanam and Mahabharatha every evening in the pedestal outside their house. The ladies of the house would be listening to this from inside the house. The lady relative thought to herself that the scholarly response which he gave her was borne out of such discourses he conducted. She laughed to herself and prayed to Allah that peace be restored and for the two families to be united soon.

World War II began on September 1, 1939. It also affected India which at that time was under the subjugation of the British. Leaders who dreamt of an independent India actively participated in the freedom movement at the time. Electricity was distributed for the first time in Rameswaram during this period. The Sethupathi rulers of Ramanathapuram had arranged for two generators for the electric power distribution in their town. As it was distributed from the temple, the people referred to it as 'temple current.' The children played happily under the street lights. Young Abdul Kalam also enjoyed it with the others.

As the children were turning into adults, marriage proposals were discussed. Jain Maraikayar's sister Ayishamma approached him for the wedding of Asim Zohara with Ahmed Jallaluddin that had been fixed at the time Asim Zohara was born. Since Jain Maraikayar regarded his brother's children as his own, he was looking for a suitable match for his brother's daughter Sultan Beevi Fathima. Mohammed Maraikayar was dead. Asiyamma, who had been very close to her Chacha, wanted to restore cordial relations with his family members as before.

People who understood her good intentions, tried to establish a wedding proposal to reunite the two families. The marriage between Mohammed Maraikayar's son Abdul Zafar and Jain Maraikayar's brother's daughter was fixed. However, Abdul Zafar was adamant. He said that he would get married only after his sister Ahmed Kaniyamma got married. He also insisted that Jain Maraikayar's son Chinna Maraikka was the right match for his sister. At that time, Chinna Maraikka was very young and had no interest in getting married. He wanted to wait for a few more years. Jain Maraikayar's brother's son Samsuddin fetched him from the plantation. Chinna Maraikka had great respect for Samsuddin who was elder to him.

When he saw his elder cousin, he asked, "What happened, Kaakka? Why have you come in search of me?" He replied, "Chinna Maraikka, only if you get married to Mohammed Maraikayar's daughter, will we be able to get your sister Thangamma married. If you refuse this proposal, then you only should marry your sister. That is permitted in Islam. According to the doctrine of Islam, marriage between older/younger brothers' siblings are permitted. Do you understand?" He said this and left immediately. How could Chinna Maraikka marry Thangamma who was like his own sister to him? Wouldn't it be akin to a lame fellow looking for a suitable bride in his father's younger brother's family? After giving it much thought, Chinna Maraika finally agreed to get married to Mohammed Maraikayar's daughter Ahmed Kaniyamma.

The two families were now reunited. "Quarrels are quarrels and relationships are relationships." Mohammed Maraikayar's voice echoed there. Asiyamma was very happy that her Chacha Mohammed Maraikayar's daughter would now become her daughter-in-law. She was curious to know about her future daughter-in-law. She enquired about her to a few relatives. "Mohammed Maraikayar's daughter is a very brisk girl. She would wake up early in the morning. After bathing, she would wash her clothes and pray every day. She is a very hygienic and a responsible girl", they replied. Asiyamma felt happy to hear this.

Jain Maraikayar's mother Sultan Beevi Fathima was happy to hear about the news of her grandchildren's wedding. Wedding preparations began. Sultan Beevi Fathima called her son and reminded him of the ceremony of praying to their ancestors before the wedding. It is a tradition followed by the Maraikayar family. Whenever a male member of the family got married, they would recite the Fatiha and pray to their ancestors invoking their blessings.

Chinna Maraikka who was listening to his Vappumma (father's mom) began to recall past incidents. He thought of his Ummamma (mother's mom) Hasanachiyar and his eyes began to well up. He recalled her unconditional love towards them, the initiatives she took to complete the construction of her daughter's house, and her participation during the Sunnath ceremony...then again, her culinary skills...her onion sambar, banana puttu, pepper tomato sambar... he could inhale their aroma now even as he thought about her. He then recalled the day she passed away. On a Sunday, they invited guests and served them ghee rice with curry kuzhambu and recited the Fatiha praying to their ancestors Avul Ambalam, Pakir Ambalam, Ibrahim Maraikayar, and Hasanachiyar.

Jain Maraikayar purchased similar silk sarees, jewellery, and utensils for his daughter Asim Zohara and his brother's daughter Sultan Beevi Fathima also known as Thangamma for their wedding. The three weddings were about to happen on the same night. Relatives from the bride and the bridegroom's families were summoned to install the first posts for the marriage pandal. A seven-foot long palm stick was chosen and painted white. Mango leaves and jasmine flowers were tied to the top portion of this stick. On the western side, a deep hole was dug and the eldest male member of the family inserted the stick first followed by the others. Turmeric paste was applied to this stick from the eldest to the youngest. They recited the Fatiha and distributed tea and sugar-candy. They printed the wedding invitations in Madurai and distributed them to their relatives. Relatives from Pamban arrived in bullock carts. Relatives from Mandapam, Vedalai and Maraikayar Pattinam also arrived. They decorated the wedding venue beautifully. It was 'Mehandi day' for the brides. They summoned all their female relatives for this ceremony.

They tied a silk cloth to the mortar, filled it with paddy and asked the bride to grind it with the pestle first followed by the other ladies. They made the bride sit in a comfortable chair. The eldest lady (whose husband was still alive) was summoned and she put the jewellery and the mehandi for the bride. They recited the Fatiha in the name of Fathima Nachiyar, daughter of Prophet Muhammad (Peace Be Upon Him) and did the Duwah for a happy married life. They then distributed the sugar-candy. Sultan Beevi Fathima said that once the wedding date was fixed, the bride should not leave the house. She made sure that her granddaughters rested inside the house. The colour of the mehandi was identical to the colour of the faces of the coy brides.

The next morning, they applied a mixture of ghee and sandal paste to the bridegrooms. The mixture was kept ready in a cup. The relatives made the bridegrooms sit in comfortable chairs and applied this mixture to their heads while chanting 'Bismi.' Then they all came to the bride's family and applied this mixture chanting 'Bismi.' The three brides and bridegrooms bathed, did the Wudu ritual and got ready for the wedding. Abdul Zafar was adamant that since his father was no more, he would sit in his place and hand over his sister to her life partner. Therefore, the wedding of the youngest couple Ahmed Kaniyamma and Chinna Maraikka happened first. Chinna Maraikka was clad in a maroon coat which was stitched in Madurai. He wore a wedding garland. The procession of the bridegroom started with the chanting 'Laa Ilaha Illallah...'. The bridegroom was made to sit in a car. Sultan Maraikayar's son Ibrahim Maraikayar accompanied him as the 'bridegroom's friend.'

In order to greet the bridegroom, the men and the children from the relatives' family stood with garlands and milk in their hands. When the car stopped near their house, they garlanded the bridegroom and offered milk to him. When they reached the bride's house, brother-in-law Abdul Zafar garlanded the bridegroom and welcomed them. They made the bridegroom sit on the pandal facing west. Pesh Imam Hajiyar Shahul Hamid and other elders of the mosque sat on the stage where the Nikkah (wedding) was about to happen. The Nikkah book was brought to register the wedding formally. This book contained columns like Wedding day, Time, Name of the bride, Name of the bridegroom, their respective fathers' names, and witnesses. The bridegroom laid his signature on the concerned page.

The bride's agreement to the wedding and her signature were received by two relatives who took the book to the place where she was sitting. Pesh Imam started the festivities and gave a lecture on the importance of marriage. "With witnesses by my side, for a hundred and one 'Mahar' (the bridegroom has to give this sum to the bride), I am giving the hand of T.S. Mohammed Maraikayar's daughter T.S.M. Ahmed Kaniyamma in marriage to you as your lawfully wedded wife. Do you agree?", he asked the bridegroom three times. After agreement, they did the Duwah and the wedding ceremony happened.

Betel leaves, flowers and the 'mangalsutra' chain made with black beads and corals in a golden strand were kept on a tray and circulated among the elders to receive their blessings for the wedding. While Pesh Imam did the Duwah, the eldest female member (whose husband was still alive) tied the chain to the bride. Abdul Zafar brought Chinna Maraikka to the wedding platform and seated him next to his sister Ahmed Kaniyamma. He then joined their hands together. The ladies made a noise (known as 'kulavai') to announce the wedding. Now that he had performed his duty successfully, Abdul Zafar decorated himself as a bridegroom and got ready for his wedding. With his younger brothers on his side, he did a procession. He then got married to Thangammal. After this, the wedding between Asim Zohara and Ahmed Jallaluddin happened. They had a feast with ghee rice and curry kurma. With the blessings of their near and dear ones, the three weddings happened smoothly. The Nadhaswaram and Ketti Melam instrumentalists were delighted to play for their boss's family wedding events.

After their wedding ceremony got over, the bridegrooms got back to their respective homes. The people from the bride's families invited them for breakfast the following day. The bridegrooms wearing silk dhotis and silk shirts went to the respective bride's houses and received a warm welcome. They made different snacks and savouries everyday for the bride and the groom. Snacks like laddus and poli were made. They made 'Wattalappam' out of a hundred eggs and gave it to the bridegroom and his family.

On the fifth day, they had to take a head bath. They announced to their relatives that the ceremony will happen around 7 PM. Hot water was kept ready for bathing in the brides' families. The relatives arrived. After their formal head bath in their respective homes, the grooms arrived with their relatives. The eldest lady (whose husband was alive) led them. They brought with them shikakai powder, fragrance powder (for hair), oil, mirror, comb, sweets, greengram, banana plantains, puffed rice, groundnuts, beaten rice, betel leaves, betel nuts and flowers on eleven trays. The paddy which was kept at the time of fixing the date was made into rice and then mixed with gram dal, jaggery and coconut to prepare sweetened milk rice. The fragrant powder was mixed with soft sandal powder and kept ready in a cup. The bride and the groom were made to sit on comfortable chairs. The oldest person applied the oil on their heads. The rest of the relatives followed him. The bridegroom's brothers-in-law and friends teased and made him take an oil bath. He then wore the new silk dresses.

Likewise, the bride was also made to take the oil bath, after which she wore her new silk saree. The sweetened milk rice was then fed to the bride and the groom. Next, coins were laid out in 'Pallankuzhi' (a game played using cowries) and the game began. The relatives of the groom surrounded him and those of the bride surrounded her. They started playing. While playing they teased one another and enjoyed themselves. Those who lost, won and those who won, lost. Isn't this the philosophy of life as well? On the seventh day, the brides had to leave for their respective husbands' houses.

During any ceremony of the Maraikayar family, it was customary to bring palanquins from the Devasthanam. Jain Maraikayar said that Ahmed Kaniyamma had to be brought to her husband's family first. That girl who was just thirteen years old left for her husband's house wearing her mangalsutra and head filled with dreams. A huge pot filled with water was kept at the entrance of the house. Her mom Peerammal gave her a bronze chest, kissed her forehead and bade farewell to her daughter Ahmed Kaniyamma. With tears in her eyes, she then bid farewell to her little brothers and elder sisters. As the relatives gave them coins inside betel leaves, the chest became full. After touching the water kept in the pot, the bride and the groom chanted

'Bismillah' and left. Along with them, Abdul Kalam too sat inside the palanquin.

The palanquin bearers safely carried them to Jain Maraikayar's house. Asiyamma took the 'Arati' to the newlyweds. "Put your right foot forward and come in chanting Bismillah", she told her bride. They gave milk and fruits to the newlyweds. Little boy Abdul Kalam was enjoying all this. He closely observed all the events. Ahmed Kaniyamma was taken to the kitchen. They asked her to insert her hand in the rice pot, salt pot and so on. "From now on, you are a part of our family and let everything you touch become auspicious"-this was the symbolic meaning behind this. Was this ritual done to convey their heart's wishes or was it just a mere custom? This little boy couldn't understand all that at such a young age. Running beside his mother, he kept on enquiring about the meaning of all these rituals. Likewise, Asim Zohara and Thangamma were taken to their respective husband's houses.

On the ninth day, once again they were taken to their husband's houses. As per the Maraikayar family tradition, it was decided that the next day they should all go to the Dargah. They started to get ready from early morning onwards in the brides' houses. They made rotis from rice flour. They made Kozhukattai. Multipurpose fragrant powder was kept ready. They prepared milk rice. The newlyweds wore silk garments. They fetched the bullock carts and tied a cloth to shield the bride and other ladies. They all then left for the Dargah.

They took them to the Habil-Qabil Dargah, recited the Fatiha and did the Duwah for the well-being of the newlyweds. They put some money in the Hundi. They then handed over the fragrant powder to the brides and asked them to sprinkle it under the mother's coffin. They then went to the burial places of their ancestors to pray. The huge banyan tree that gave shade to the father's coffin drew the attention of young Abdul Kalam and his friends. They played swinging in the aerial roots.

After they did the Duwah near the father's coffin and Mohaideen Peer's coffin, they distributed the food items like rotis, Kozhukattai and so on which they brought with them. They drew water from the Dargah well, did the Wudu ritual and prayed. They climbed on their bullock carts and reached their respective homes by nightfall. The brides were taken to the houses of their respective bridegrooms on the fifteenth day of their marriage. Inside bronze pots, brass vessels, pots of different types, coloured container boxes were kept 1001 'Seepu Paniyaram' and 1001 'Adhirasam' and were covered with turmeric-coated white clothes. With the rest of the items like betel leaves, betel nuts, flowers, banana plantains and so on, the brides were taken to the respective bridegroom's houses. After this, the Paniyaram, Adhirasam and fruits were kept inside straw boxes and distributed to their relatives. It was also distributed to other near and dear ones.

The newlywed couples were given a feast in their relatives' homes. Days turned into weeks, and weeks turned into months. Ahmed Kaniyamma settled down well in Jain Maraikayar's house. Abdul Kalam was very fond of his brother's wife and would address her as 'Machi.' He never left her side. When there was no electricity, he would ask her to accompany him to the backyard. Ahmed Kaniyamma was also very affectionate towards her brother-in-law. Asiyamma was proud of her daughter-in-law.

It was time for the temple festivities. They invited Jain Maraikayar to construct the boats for the float festival. Along with his talented worker Maidavul, he made the necessary arrangements. After the festivity, as usual, Jain Maraikayar went to the temple to receive the honours. His young son Abdul Kalam also accompanied him. Kalam noticed everything that happened. When his Machi asked him, "Did you go and see?" Kalam described everything he saw vividly. Ahmed Kani had heard about the temple honours. After Kalam's description, she understood clearly. When young Ahmed Kaniyamma became pregnant, the entire Maraikayar family became excited. Sultan Beevi Fathima took great care of her grandson's wife. Lemon and mango pickles were made. Everyone bought various food items suitable for a pregnant woman. Looking at her stout belly, Abdul Kalam would mock her, "Why is the tummy of this Ganapati so big?" Jain Maraikayar was looking for a suitable bride for his younger brother's son Samsuddin. They decided that Pamban Munsif Meerasa Maraikayar's elder brother's daughter Saharban would be a perfect match. After the 'Maghrib' prayer, the elders left for Pamban to fix the alliance. Young Abdul Kalam also went along. They reached home at night.

The next morning, Machi Ahmed Kanima asked Kalam, "Did you see the girl?" to which he replied, "Yes, Machi. The girl had fair skin However, there were dots all over her face." Listening to their conversation, Sultan Beevi Fathima asked her grandson, "What are you saying?" Asiyamma replied, "He is simply making fun of his Kaakka's wife. The girl was struck with measles last month. That is the reason behind those dots." Ahmed Kani was surprised to hear the way in which Kalam decently described them to be spots. Peerammal came during the seventh month to take her daughter Ahmed Kaniyamma with her to her house for delivery. Surrounded by their relatives, carrying the usual items like fruits, sweets and savouries, they brought Ahmed Kaniyamma to her mother's house during the first week of her seventh month after she had received blessings from the elders of the house. When Chinna Maraikka went to pray, Shahul Hamid Hajiyar told him, "You will be blessed with a baby boy, Chinna Maraikka". Smilingly, Chinna Maraikka replied, "If that happens, I will name him after you."

In the tenth month, a handsome baby boy was born. They named him 'Shahul Hamid.' After this, Thangammal also gave birth to a baby boy who was named as 'Mohammed Jamaldin.' Ahmed Jallaluddin left his pregnant wife Asim Zohara with his mother Ayishamma to Columbo to earn. The lady relatives gathered around her during her delivery. She was suffering from labour pain for nearly three days. The baby wouldn't come out even after several attempts made by the midwives. They then went to the government hospital to bring the lady doctor. The doctor came to attend to her delivery. After she applied Chloroform, the doctor used medical instruments to aid the birth. Finally, Asima delivered a baby girl. The doctor had come the previous night and the baby got delivered at 4.15 AM the next day.

The relatives rushed to fetch the money that had to be given to the lady doctor. Chinna Maraikka was very happy that his beloved sister had survived and so handed over 101 silver coins. On a huge tray, they then kept the money along with fruits and coconut and gave it to the doctor. They named the girl as 'Avul Mahaboob Begum.' Now that the children were born, there was happiness all over. Cradles were prepared for Shahul Hamid, Mohammed Jamaldin, and Mahaboob in Jain Maraikayar's house portico. While one was awake, the other would be asleep. Days and nights went in this way. Next was Samsuddin's wedding ceremony. They went by train and bullock cart, and

Saharban returned with all of them soon after the marriage. The family members rejoiced over their wedding.

The people in Rameswaram were afraid of the impact of World War II. Since Rameswaram was close to Sri Lanka, people were scared that the Britishers might bomb Rameswaram. Slowly, those people who were not native to Rameswaram started to leave the place. Those who belonged to the place left it all to God and continued on their daily routine. At the time of the war, there was a food shortage. The people were asked to switch off the lights before 7 PM. In case of a bomb, bunkers were set up by the Jilla office department. The local people also helped them and earned some money out of this.

Since there was a shortage of raw rice, people had to turn to wheat flour for cooking. Abdul Zafar, who was sick for a while, passed away leaving behind his children. Thangamma became a widow at a very young age and wore a white saree. The Maraikayar family lamented over their condition. They tried to get her remarried. However, Thangamma refused.

When bombs hit Japan in 1945, World War II came to an end. The people were shocked to hear the tragic tales of the war.

Ahmed Kaniyamma's child Thangarani was just a little infant. At the time, Ahmed Kanima had to manage all the household chores all by herself. Looking at her discomfort,

Sultan Beevi Fathima asked her to hand over her grandson's daughter to her so that she could carry on with her chores freely. Ahmed Kanima wasn't sure of this since Sultan Beevi Fathima was hardly able to move out of her place. She was afraid that the baby might slip out of the elderly lady's hand. She hesitantly handed over the child to the old lady. Ahmed Kanima (Kaniyamma was fondly known as Kanima) had one eye on her work and her other eye on the little one. Looking at her distress, the experienced Sultan Beevi Fathima said, "Hey, Mohammed's daughter! Are you scared that I might drop the infant? Don't be!" She asked her not to worry. Ahmed Kanima was a bit embarrassed that the old lady had understood her feelings. She however felt that she would now hold on to the infant more tightly and felt relieved.

The Kothandaramar temple was situated two miles away from Rameswaram. It is believed that Vibheeshana, who didn't like the character of his elder brother Ravana, left him for good, surrendered to Sri Rama in this place and joined Rama's army. A temple was erected here for Lord Sri Rama holding his divine weapon 'Kothandam' to mark this incident from the epic Ramayanam. In the Tamil month 'Maasi' (roughly mid-Feb to mid-March), Sri Ramanathaswamy from the Rameswaram temple would come on a procession to this temple annually. The devotees would throng to get a darshan of the Lord here during that time.

When he heard that the construction was about to happen in the Kothandaramar temple, Jain Maraikayar took responsibility for it. He took charge of the 'temple contract' by appointing suitable people and supervised the project. After his morning 'Fajr' prayer, he left with a bronze jar filled with water and a box of greengram laddus. He would be back home right in time for the 'Dhuhr' prayer everyday. He would satisfy his hunger by eating the laddus and drinking water. He kept a close watch on the temple project. The workers too happily received the laddus and worked hard.

Even though all the Maraikayar children were sent to school, only Abdul Kalam and Noordeen showed interest in studying. Samsuddin Maraikayar bought and distributed the 'Dinamani' newspaper throughout the town. He was therefore known as 'The newspaper man' by everyone. Every morning, Abdul Kalam would accompany him to fetch the newspaper that would have arrived by train; over time, since Samsuddin had to open his shop on time, Abdul Kalam alone would go to the railway station to fetch the paper and both of them would then arrange them; later, Abdul Kalam would distribute the newspapers to various homes. Since Kalam was fond of reading, he enjoyed this regular routine. His brother would give some money for his services.

Noordeen and Abdul Kalam completed their primary schooling in the local elementary school. For Higher secondary education, it was decided that they should be sent to Ramanathapuram. The children felt sad that they had to leave the house and study elsewhere. However, out of interest for studying and based on their teachers' advice, they decided to leave. Kalam's mother, who was very fond of him, couldn't bear this separation. However, she made all necessary arrangements for travel since this would help her son to become a great man some day. She kept his washed and neatly laundered clothes inside a trunk box. The books and pens were also kept in the box. He had to leave the next morning by train. Ahmed Kanima filled a bronze jar with water from the well and closed it with a betel leaf. She left it at the house entrance. They all prayed while Kalam left the house for his well-being.

Chinna Maraikka handed over an unbroken turmeric tuber to Jain Maraikayar while Kalam's grandmother, mother, father, brothers, Machi, and other children were watching. Jain Maraikayar dipped the turmeric tuber in the water in the jar and wrote the following verses from the Holy Qur'an on the house wall, "Innal lazee farada 'alaikal Qur-aana laraaadduka ilaa ma'ad..." which means, "Verily, He Who has given you the Qur'an will surely bring you back to your house of residence."(28:85, 86). Jain Maraikayar recited this verse and asked his son Kalam to recite it after him. He prayed to God to protect his son. Kalam's mother gave money for his travel and hugged him tightly. After he bid his farewell to everyone, he dipped his hands in the jar and wiped away his tears, left in pursuit of a bright future.

Abdul Kalam started his education in Schwartz Higher Secondary School in Ramanathapuram. He missed his family and they all missed him very much. Ahmed Kanima missed her brother-in-law very much. She recalled Kalam's childhood pranks. They used to tie the greengram laddus in a pot kept high up, and out of reach of the children. Abdul Kalam would secretly come there while his mother was sleeping. He would put a chair and take a handful of them. On his way out, he would ask Machi not to inform his mother. 'Would he have eaten properly today?' Ahmed Kanima thought to herself. All her thoughts were with Kalam who was now staying inside the Schwartz hostel.

Asiyamma gave a straw box to Ahmed Kaniyamma who was thinking only about her brother-in-law. She then gave her instructions to fry the cat-fish. Ahmed Kanima recalled her childhood memories of the Panchakalyani river and the tamarind plantations on its banks. She started preparing the fish curry as instructed. However, her mind was thinking about the story of the river that she had heard from others...

Till 1480, Rameswaram was a part of the country's mainland. However, after a severe storm, it became an island surrounded by sea water on all sides. To the south of Rameswaram island is the Devakuli river and to the north is the Panchakalyani river. Devakuli river was situated near the Nambu Nayaki Amman temple. Panchakalyani river runs from Poovarasankulam till the first sector of Narikuzhy. Tamarind trees grew in abundance here. The families of Mohammed Maraikayar and Jain Maraikayar owned tamarind plantations in this region. They appointed labourers to take care of the tamarind plantations. Kanima was recalling incidents from her childhood when she used to accompany her father to those plantations. She now started to prepare gravy out of the fish.

Jain Maraikayar was fond of fish curry. In particular, curry made out of cat-fish from the Panchakalyani river was a special delicacy. They would ask Raj Ambalam, who was in-charge of the tamarind plantation to catch some cat-fish. As soon as he brought the fish, they cleaned it, made gravy and the spawn was fried. This was a regular recipe in the Maraikayar family.

While Abdul Kalam was standing in the playground of the Schwartz School, someone called out to him. “Kalam, you have a visitor.” It was Mona Pena also known as Mo. Periyakaruppan Ambalam who was a dear friend to Chinna Maraikka. He would enquire about Kalam’s well-being. “I have informed your Kaakka before leaving. Here are some special snacks from the Ervadi Santhana Koodu festival. Share this with your other friends and eat.” He would then hand over a bag filled with savouries to Kalam.

Mona Pena was a frequent visitor there. His brother's friend became a good friend to Kalam as well.

Sultan Beevi Fathima, who couldn't move around as before, suddenly became ill. She realised that these were her last days. Holding her son's hands, she recited "La Ilaha Illallah..." and breathed her last.

Political happenings around the world created an impact in India. The Labour party won in England and they decided to give independence to India. However, India had to be partitioned. This became unavoidable. Therefore, Pakistan was created one day before August 15, 1947 when India got her independence. The national leaders spoke on the radio. People listened to them eagerly. They read the newspapers and got to know of the information. The Union Jack Flag (this was the flag indicative of the union of England, Scotland and Ireland) was brought down and India's tri-colour flag was raised.

Abdul Kalam, who was a school student, felt very happy to hear news of India's independence. He collected news related to it and read them eagerly. He did this day and night. He would read various news articles related to India's independence and felt very happy.

India was partitioned soon after independence. The worst calamity struck northern regions of India on account of the clash between religions. Refugee crisis also started. Several lakhs of people were affected due to this. Mahatma

Gandhi, the Father of the Nation, also lost his life. He was shot to death. People of the nation were heart broken. He, who fought for India's independence, was unable to live for a long time after independence! A government had to be formed under such critical circumstances.

Jawaharlal Nehru became the first Prime Minister of India. The Constitution of India was established. Various government bodies were established all over India. The Panchayat boards were established for maintaining the towns. Jain Maraikayar was chosen as the Panchayat head. Before independence, people had to pay house tax, and plantation tax. With the establishment of the new constitution, the people's representatives had to now collect wealth tax, maintain the streets, and clean their respective localities.

Jain Maraikayar was the 'Muthavalli' (people who took the lead role in maintaining the mosque for several generations in a row) of the mosque. Now he was also the chairman of the town council. The people were happy to have their beloved Jain Maraikayar as their leader.

Pilgrims from all over the world came to Rameswaram, visit Dhanushkodi, otherwise known as 'Adam's Bridge.' They had to travel in small boats to reach Dhanushkodi. Jain Maraikayar's family also owned small boats that were used for this purpose. They appointed boatmen and earned money by transporting passengers to and from Dhanushkodi. After their morning prayer rituals, they sailed along with the pilgrims in their boats and took them to get a darshan of Dhanushkodi. Chinna Maraikka was fond of this business. He learnt various languages like Malayalam, Telugu, Kannada and other Indian languages on account of this. He decided to build a shop near this place. He therefore built one near the piece of land next to Savukkai the Maraikayar family owned near the Eenjiyadippa Dargah. The provision store was opened in the Keppai Vadi corner. Jain Maraikayar wanted to use large boats for transportation in the Rameswaram-Dhanushkodi zone. A small boat could accommodate only twelve passengers, whereas a big boat could accommodate at least thirty passengers.

In order to get a big boat, Jain Maraikayar travelled to Thopputhurai in Pudukottai district. To reach there, he used the Thopputhurai boat that was used on a rental basis for fishing in Rameswaram waters. Even though a friend had accompanied him, his family members were concerned for his well-being. Telephone facility wasn't available back then. His family members missed him very much. Jain Maraikayar bought the rental boats from Thopputhurai. They said that they could only rent it out and refused to sell the boats. Even though he had failed in his mission, he loaded huge coconuts from there in his boat on his way back to Rameswaram. There were heavy rains. Somehow, he managed to bring the coconuts safely and sold them.

He worked hard to fulfil his dream of owning a big boat. He started constructing one with the help of good carpenters. They chose the best wood for this purpose. The job was completed within a month. Pamban port issued a 'Permit licence' for boats back then. A Port officer would come everyday and give the ticket for boat transport permit.

Jain Maraikayar named his boat as 'Pamban Port Boat No. 91' and registered it under the names of his wife Asiyamma and his brother's wife Alima Ammal. Half of the money he earned was given to his workers and the rest was shared among his brother's children.

It was a hot summer day. Students were having their lunch in Schwartz School. Mona Pena rushed to the place to see Abdul Kalam. He said, "Have you eaten your lunch? I heard that you had to pay the school fees", and took out the money from his wallet. Fish scales also fell out of his wallet. Kalam was surprised to see this. "Since they told me that it was urgent, I rushed directly from the seashore where I had gone for collection", said Mona Pena and handed over the fee money to Kalam. After handing out his commodity to the fish sellers, he had rushed directly to help his dear friend's brother. Young Kalam thanked Periya Karuppan for his kindness. He realised the value of true friendship.

He recalled Thiruvalluvar's famous verse: "The merit of kindness shown by those who help without expecting a return, is vaster than the sea."

After completing his school education, Abdul Kalam wanted to pursue further studies in college. He had to complete his Intermediate course. Jain Maraikayar was looking for a suitable college. The French priest, Father Fodale, who learnt Tamil at the local Church and served there, was his good friend. (A French priest, Fodale had come to France to spread Christianity. He became close to the native people of Rameswaram. He was known as 'Fodale priest' and gave discourses at the local Church. The place where he stayed is known today as 'Fodale Complex.' He was capable of understanding Tamil and maintained a cordial relationship with Jain Maraikayar.) While they both met, he asked, "What's the matter?" Jain Maraikayar discussed Kalam's college education. "You can get him admitted to St. Joseph's College in Trichy", the priest suggested. The next day the priest gave him a recommendation letter for Kalam's admission. Jain Maraikayar and Chinna Maraikka took Kalam to Trichy. Many people had come by car to get their children admitted. These two, who had gone on a cycle rickshaw, handed the letter of recommendation from Father Fodale to the receptionist.

Within the next five minutes, Kalam got enrolled for the Intermediate course. They now made arrangements for the college admission; they kept the doctor's certificate ready; they had to get this from a lady doctor in Madurai who was a surgeon. Periya Karuppan Ambalam accompanied Abdul Kalam to Madurai. Peer Ravuthar who lived in a place called 'Aattumanthai' accompanied them and they got the doctor's certificate. After completing his Intermediate studies, Kalam wanted to pursue his B.Sc. course there. In time, Jain Maraikayar's younger brother's son Mahmood Abu Baker got a baby boy; he was named 'Mohammed Ibrahim' after his brother.

The days passed. It was not time for the Navratri festival at the Rameswaram temple. The Navratri festivities happened every year for twelve days. People from north India visited Rameswaram to witness this celebration. Thc entire town celebrated. The mantras recited from the temple reverberated all over the place.

Business flourished during this time in all the shops. 'Serpadi' is a kind of measure used in north India. This is slightly less than 1 Kg. Veerabathra Nayakkar and Govinda Nayakkar used this measure in their shops. The north Indians bought provision items such as flour, oil and so on from their shops and cooked in their accommodation. The Navratri festivities came to an end.

The wheel of time was spinning. Jain Maraikayar was now the Panchayat President; he was referred to as 'President' and 'leader' by one and all; his son Chinna Maraikka was appointed as the Bench Court Magistrate; this was perhaps to indicate that the Maraikayar family was respected by the people in their hometown.

It was now time for the Katchatheevu festivities. The Palk Strait situated between Rameswaram and Thalai Mannar was rich in fish. Expensive fish varieties such as sharks, seal fish, anchovies, as well as prawns, crabs, shrimps, sting rays were found there in abundance. In this zone, Katchatheevu is located 10 miles to the northeast midway between Rameswaram and TalaiMannar. Therefore, fishermen from Tamil Nadu went all the way upto west of Sri Lanka beyond Katchatheevu to catch the fish. Sri Lankan fishermen would come up till Dhanushkodi to catch the fish.

In Katchatheevu, the fishermen from Tamil Nadu and Sri Lanka rested, repaired their boats and dried their fishing nets. In this rich land, was the Church of St. Antony, who was the protector of the Roman Catholic fishermen. Every March, St. Antony's festival happened here; without any passport and visa, thousands of people from India and Sri Lanka attended this festival. During this festival, the relatives from both these nations were therefore free to interact in this island with one another without the need to oblige to any rules or regulations; marriage proposals were fixed during this time; items that were rare in Sri Lanka such as small onions, pulses, cotton clothes and so on were given from India and coconuts from Masi and Jaffna, Rani soap and electronic items were brought from there; the drumsticks of Jaffna are very lengthy and people would cut a piece of the stick and bring it to India; by the time of the following year's celebrations, these sticks that were laid would have started to yield little drumsticks.

Passengers from Rameswaram travelled in boats and stayed there for three days; on account of travellers coming from all parts of India during this time, Rameswaram town would be buzzing with activity. Chinna Maraikka was eager to visit Katchatheevu; after getting permission from his parents, he travelled with fellow passengers on his boat, attended the St. Antony's festival and returned back home in the evening. He bought soaps and chocolates and distributed them to his relatives; he would narrate the stories of his visit to his friends and relatives.

Jain Maraikayar who had a stiff body and sharp eyes was an intelligent man who resolved all disputes in the local Panchayat; he always served justice to those who approached him. Therefore, people always stood by his judgement. He was able to identify the guilty person with the help of evidence. One time, thieves had stolen rice and other goods from the shop by removing the roof. As Jain Maraikayar was inspecting the footprints in the place, he asked the people who had recently built their huts nearby. "Why did you do this? I see that even your wife had been an accomplice", he said. "Please forgive us, master", said the thief. As he was about to fall at his feet, Jain Maraikayar stopped him and sent him away.

His friend asked Jain Maraikayar, "How did you identify the culprit correctly?" He replied, "The footprints ended in their house from the spot where the roof had been removed. Those footprints belonged to a woman with her footring. Therefore, I deduced that the husband had removed the items by removing the roof and the wife had collected them from below." Jain Maraikayar was not only efficient in identifying footprints on land, but also on water; one morning, he realised while he visited the coconut plantation, that a few coconuts were stolen; as he went around the coconut trees, he followed the footprints underneath. Even as he had walked 2-3 feet, he noticed little potholes formed out of rain water.

His friend wondered how Jain Maraikayar could possibly identify the man who had crossed these potholes; Jain Maraikayar lifted his dhoti and walked along a path that was filled with water; the water patch ended at a distance; the two swam across to the other side; there was a hut! When they both stood outside, an old lady approached them: "Master, please forgive us. My son made a mistake", she said.

When he enquired further, she said, "Yesterday, my daughter-in-law gave birth to twins. Due to rain, we couldn't earn anything. That was why he stole those coconuts. See them over there." She showed him inside the house. Without giving her a reply, he handed over some money to her and said, "This is for the infants." "Master! Please name my babies", her daughter-in-law rushed to him. "Allah! Please bless these infants", prayed Jain Maraikayar and named them as Lakshmi and Parvati and blessed them.

"How were you able to identify the hut that was so far away?" asked his friend out of curiosity. "I could see smoke at a distance. That's why I went there. The man who stole our coconuts might have seen us. He could have possibly warned his mother and left. It's alright. Just leave it", replied Jain Maraikayar.

It was an annual vacation for Abdul Kalam; He came to his hometown. He visited the mosque, prayed and recited the Holy Qur'an; however, he wanted to make sure that he recited the verses correctly; he conveyed his wish to his father; his father felt that 'Asan Bhava' was the right person for this; he was Abu Baker's ('Avvakkarappa's') younger sister's husband. He ran a business in Malaysia. He had also come on a visit to their hometown during the holiday season. Upon Jain Maraikayar's request, starting from the alphabets 'Alif', 'Be' and so on, he taught the proper recitation of the Holy Qur'an to young Abdul Kalam; Kalam learnt this with utmost dedication.

Abdul Kalam resumed his college studies; even during these days, he received several notes of money with fish scales intertwined; Periya Karuppan Ambalam was a frequent visitor who came to enquire about Kalam's well-being. Periya Karuppan Ambalam and Pazhanivel Nadar provided financial assistance for Kalam's studies; Pazhanivel Nadar accepted the repayment; however, Periya Karuppan would refuse to take back his money; the Maraikayar family had to force him to take back his money.

With the help of kind-hearted people, Kalam completed his B.Sc; he also got an appointment letter from the Ilayangudi Dr. Zakir Hussain college. However, Abdul Kalam had other ideas. He told his father and brothers that he wanted to study further; since they approved, he joined the engineering course in M.I.T. (Madras Institute of Technology).

The cordial relations between the Sethupathi kings of Ramanathapuram and Rameswaram Maraikayar family continued for generations; Whenever Shanmuganatha Sethupathi came to Rameswaram to have a darshan of Ramanathaswamy, he always visited Jain Maraikayar; before he arrived, his bookkeeper would announce to Jain Maraikayar, "The king will be visiting you. He wanted me to inform you of his arrival." Jain Maraikayar made sure that he was always present whenever the Sethupathi king came to his home. Muthusamy worked in Rameswaram Samasthanam; he also conveyed messages from the Sethupathi king to Maraikayar.

Abdul Kalam wanted to study in M.I.T.; Jain Maraikayar went to Chennai to meet his friend, the Sethupathi king; he was a member of the Tamil Nadu state ministry at the time. When he saw Jain Maraikayar, he asked, "Why have you come this far? You could have sent word through Muthusamy or Karunanantham (Dewan), right?" When Jain Maraikayar informed him about the purpose of his visit, "You get back to your hometown. We will take care of it", said the king. He asked someone to buy the train ticket for his return and handed it over to Jain Maraikayar. Jain Maraikayar returned the next morning by the 7 AM train; by the time he had finished his bath and breakfast, at around 10 AM, the enrollment letter from M.I.T. had arrived; he reached Chennai by the 12 PM afternoon train.

Now they had to pay the college fees; it was a huge sum; Periya Karuppan Ambalam was not in town at the time; he was thinking of a solution. The family members were discussing the matter. Asim Zohara immediately removed her golden bangles which were given by her family members at the time of her wedding. That fetched the money for the college fees.

Abdul Kalam bade farewell to his family, friends and relatives and came to Chennai to pursue his education in M.I.T. Abdul Kalam, who always looked up at the sky to catch a glimpse of the flying birds, joined the 'Aeronautical Engineering' course.

During the holiday season, he would come home with his college friends. He introduced them to his parents and other family members. Ahmed Kanima prepared fish curry and Kalam would serve his guests.

After completing his engineering course, Kalam joined Hindustan Aeronautics Limited (HAL) in Bangalore. He got trained to be an aeronautical engineer over there. He sent his first salary to his father and got his blessings; next, he retrieved the bangles of his beloved sister.

Asiyamma's father Mohammed Muthu Meera Lebbai Maraikayar had pledged the properties of his elder brother Sahib Maraikayar also known as Mohammed Meera Lebbai Maraikayar, his younger brother Sultan Maraikayar whom Asiyamma fondly addressed as Chacha to get loans. On account of this, they were about to lose the houses of Asiyamma's father and his elder brother. They were about to auction their homes. No one wanted to get those houses through auction since it was where the great Maraikayar family had lived; Jain Maraikayar and his mom's younger sister's son Shahul Hamid Maraikayar got back their mom's property by purchasing it. The properties were now shared by them. Asiyamma's father's ancestral home and half of the huge mansion that was built by Sahib Maraikayar now came to Jain Maraikayar. They repaired the old houses. Other than the house that he was currently living in, Jain Maraikayar built two more houses which were now ready for occupation. He summoned Ahmed Kanima.

"Kanima, both the houses are ready now? Where shall we live?" he asked her. "This house itself is enough", she replied. He said, "OK", and left. He felt that if he lived closer to the mosque, he might be able to hear the prayer calls easily. Asiyamma, who understood her husband's intentions, made the necessary arrangements. She chose the north-facing house in which she was born and which was very close to the mosque. She then arranged for whitewashing the house.

Her daughter-in-law, who understood her mother-in-law's mind very well, kept ready all necessary utensils, salt, tamarind and other items. On an auspicious day, Jain Maraikayar, his wife Asiyamma, and sons Mustafa Kamal and Kasim Mohammed shifted to their new house. Everyday Chinna Maraikka brought fresh fish to his dad and mom; at times, Kanima prepared fish curry and sent it to them. There were also times when everyone wanted to eat food prepared by Kanima. They would all then stay at Chinna Maraikka's house to taste the delicacies prepared by Ahmed Kanima.

After Abdul Kalam joined HAL in Bangalore, he wanted to invite his father to stay with him over there for a few days. Jain Maraikayar visited his son in Bangalore; he used to live, eat and converse with his dear son and spent those days happily; he would pray at the local mosque in Bangalore. On Fridays, father and son would go for the Juma prayer.

Kalam would take his father to a renowned doctor for regular health check-ups and would buy all the medicines prescribed; he did an eye test and bought him spectacles. It was time for Jain Maraikayar to return back to Rameswaram. With a heavy heart, he bid farewell to his dear son Abdul Kalam. He distributed the various gifts bought by Kalam to all his relatives from his brother's and sisters' families and friends back home.

Someone called out, "Master!" Chinna Maraikka went to look at who had arrived. With fish scales all over their bodies and tired faces on account of sailing, the captain of their boat (they are called as 'Boat Thandayal') Abdul Hamid, Anaiyan and Rasa had come there. "Where have you been?" enquired Chinna Maraikka. "We heard that a lot of fish were there and went out to fish. We caught a lot of fish in our fishing nets", they announced. "Ok, now you all go and eat", said Chinna Maraikka to all of them.

When he saw Captain Abdul Hamid, he recalled past memories. When he was a young boy, Abdul Hamid was known by the name Muniyandi; he was Anaiyan's cousin (father's sister's son); he greatly helped in Chinna Maraikka's shipping business; once, he had gone to Ervadi with some dry fish. Muslims living there wanted to offer a girl's hand in marriage to Muniyandi. But on one condition! He had to convert to their religion. Since Muniyandi was very close to the Maraikayar family, he had great affinity towards Islam.

Muniyandi became Abdul Hamid and got married to Magudhuma. With Jain Maraikayar's permission, Chinna Maraikka bought a piece of land for Abdul Hamid at the back of their house; Abdul Hamid and Magudhuma stayed in a hut over there.

As he was immersed in thoughts of the boatman Abdul Hamid, someone called him. "What is the matter, master?" It was their launderer Kandasamy. For generations, their family members were doing the laundry service for the Maraikayar family. Whenever Abdul Kalam's clothes had to be washed and laundered while he left for school and college, they did the laundry service. They were very loyal to the Maraikayar family.

Monsoon began in October in Rameswaram. From then until December, boat transportation was stopped and repair work happened. In December of 1964, several boats in the seashore were in a partially repaired condition. Some of them were fully repaired. Subramania Achari, who had come from Keezhakarai to do the repair work, had completed most of the job. Only a few nails had to be fitted. It was getting dark; he slept inside the boat that he was repairing. He decided to return to town the following day after finishing the rest of the work. He was not aware of what was about to happen to him!

That evening, Ahmed Kanima felt as if the breeze was all over the ground. As night approached, the speed of the wind increased greatly. Chinna Maraikka who normally chatted a while with his Kaakka Samsuddin after the night time 'Isha' prayer, had not yet returned home. Kanima could feel wet air hitting her body. She therefore served dinner early to her children and made them sleep in the hall. Chinna Maraikka returned home. After they both ate their dinner, they went to sleep with their children.

Chinna Maraikka slept on the bed in the verandah outside the main hall. He felt a wet sensation all over his body at night while sleeping. At first, as he was half asleep, he felt that it was just rain droplets trickling. He then pushed his bed slightly inside and slept. However, he couldn't. The wind whistled and blew ferociously. He saw that a lot of people had gathered on the streets; the breeze blew the night lamp as well. He couldn't understand what was happening! When sunlight was beginning to appear, he saw that the entire street was flooded. When he went and saw their backyard, the fences were ruined. The coconut trees had fallen.

Someone was screaming from outside. "Your sister's house on market street is afloat!" Chinna Maraikka was concerned. What could have happened to his sister and her daughter? He got worried. His family started to cry. A few years back, Ahmed Jallaluddin bought a house near the sea on market street and lived there with his wife and daughter. On the day of the storm, he had left the town on business. His brother Haja Mohaideen stayed back. In order to save his sister and her daughter, Chinna Maraikka had to swim across. However, several trees were uprooted in the storm.

Chinna Maraikka swam with his brother-in-law and eldest son-in-law Noordeen and his wife's brother Avul Naina via Chettiya street and Muthu Chavadi street and somehow reached the market street. The ground floor was completely flooded. Asim Zohara, Mehboob and Haja Mohaideen were standing on the first floor. He rushed to their rescue. He caught his sister with one hand and his sister's daughter with the other hand and swam with them. Avul Naina cleared the obstructions along the way.

Behind them was Noordeen, who carried the treasure chest of his brother on his head. Haja Mohaideen followed them carrying a few precious items in his hands.

Chinna Maraikka left his sister and her daughter in his aunt Ayishamma's house and went to his house fully soaked in water. The town was completely destroyed on account of the storm; Jain Maraikayar came to see his son Chinna Maraikka who had rescued his daughter and granddaughter; he was accompanied by Mustafa Kamal and Kasim Mohammed; after he learnt of their safety, Jain Maraikayar felt relieved. He then addressed his son Mustafa Kamal, "Take your brother and go to our shop. In case, there is something left there, please bring them." He came into the house to see his daughter-in-law, granddaughters and grandson.

Father and son went to the backyard; they straightened the fences as much as they could; they brought the small coconut plants that were not blown by the storm inside the house. As they were entering, Mustafa Kamal and Kasim Mohammed, who had gone to inspect their shop, returned home. "What happened" enquired their father. They showed what was left. A few packets of tea leaves, sugar and semolina were all that were left. "The storm had blown away the roof. The shop is flooded. Everything was soaked in the water. These were the only items left", they said.

Ahmed Kanima prepared tea without milk using the tea packet and sugar that was brought by her brothers-in-law. Mustafa Kamal took the hot tea in a flask to his mom, wife and children. Jain Maraikayar and Chinna Maraikka had their tea. After drinking his tea, Jain Maraikayar said to Ahmed Kanima, "Ok. Please take care of your children", and left. Ahmed Kanima distributed the flour, raw rice, eggs, coconuts, sugar and tea leaves to her in-law's house and other relatives and began to prepare breakfast.

As it dawned, the horrific news of the storm reached their ears. In the south-eastern corner of Rameswaram was Dhanushkodi. This Dhanushkodi, which remained as a holy place of pilgrimage and as a port town for over 2000 years was completely destroyed overnight on account of the storm. During World War II, this place had served as a fort as well.

The Dutch who settled along the seashore signed a treaty in 1660 CE with the Ramanathapuram Sethupathis to use the Pamban Bridge that belonged to them. They wanted to use this passage to sail their ships. Therefore, until the end of the seventeenth century, many ships sailed from the Pamban and Kundhukaal ports to Sri Lanka, Bengal and the West coast. In the beginning of the twentieth century, this port went to the British. After that, these ports got destroyed completely. Later in 1911, in order to establish port activity between Dhanushkodi and Talaimannar, the Britishers appointed German engineers.

In 1914, The British India Railway Company established boat transport and train to Chennai from this port that was situated 15 Kms from Rameswaram. Therefore, Dhanushkodi which was a sacred pilgrim spot became an important port of the British.

In southern India, Dhanushkodi became a famous sea port next to Chennai and Thoothukudi. From this port, two steam boats named 'Irwin' and 'Koshin' sailed to Talaimannar in Sri Lanka. Dhanushkodi which used to be such an important port got destroyed in the overnight storm in 1964.

Soon after the midnight of December 22, 1964 at about 12:30 AM, Dhanushkodi was swept over by the storm that approached it at 120 Km/hr. Fishermen used to describe Palk Bay as a peaceful place. Quite unexpectedly, waves that were 20 feet tall arose from Palk Bay and entered forcefully into Dhanushkodi. On account of this, temples, mandapams, hundreds of houses, railway station, government offices and other buildings in Dhanushkodi were completely destroyed. One kilometre of landmass in southern Dhanushkodi got submerged underwater. There was an enormous loss of life and property.

The train from Pamban that was approaching Dhanushkodi at midnight, got displaced from its tracks on account of the storm. The engine of the train along with seven other compartments with passengers were swept away by the sea waves. All the people including medical students who had travelled by this train lost their lives. Those ships that were parked in Rameswaram port were destroyed due to the wind and sea water; dead bodies floated all over the place; cats, sheeps, cattle, and poultry also perished.

Rescue operations began. One evening, Asiyamma came to her son Chinna Maraikka's house to see her granddaughters. Her granddaughters asked her, "Vappamma, did you hear about the storm?" She replied, "It is quite natural for the sea waves to come to the town. In order to pacify the sea, it seems there is a special pooja mantra in Rudra Veda. They pray to Varuna Deva (Water God) by keeping a kalash and recite the mantras from the Veda. They then perform special abhishekams to Ramanathaswamy. Along with the abhishekam water, they carry clean clothes, Amman's mangalsutra, blouse bit, flower garland, betel nuts, betel leaves, coconuts and fruits in a new winnow and put them in the rumbling sea.

Then only will the sea God be pacified; in our Sastri's house, they say that even as they pour in those contents into the sea, the direction of the wind changes surprisingly; even now, they have done the same ritual", Asiyamma told them. Her granddaughters who were listening to her intently asked her, "Ok, what did you do?" "I prayed to Allah and asked Duwah." She then recited and explained the meaning of her Duwah to her granddaughters.

"Allāhumma innī as'aluka khayrahā.
wa a`ūdhu bika min sharrihā.

Allāhumma innī as'aluka khayrahā. wa khayra mā fīhā. wa khayra mā ursilat bih. wa a`ūdhu bika min sharrihā. wa sharri mā fīhā. wa sharri mā ursilat bih.

Allahum Majallah Rahmatan, Va la Tajallah Adaban."

This means:

"O Allah, I ask You for the good of it, and seek refuge in You against its evil. O Allah, I ask You for the good of it, for the good of what it contains, and for the good of what is sent with it. I seek refuge in You from the evil of it, from the evil of what it contains, and from the evil that is sent with it."

The girders inside the Pamban Bridge were blown away by the storm. Therefore, rail transportation had stopped. The port office arranged for motor boats for travel to and from Rameswaram; Abdul Kalam travelled on one such boat to meet his parents, siblings and relatives; he listened to the tales of the storm from the elders and the youngsters.

Arabu Nachiyar began, "Chinnappa, due to the storm a cow slept in my saree." Kalam enquired, "What happened? Tell me." Arabu explained, "After the storm, the next morning, we opened the back door; the trees had fallen; the fences fell apart; I had tied one of my sarees in the hanger outside; that had fallen down in the wind; as the fence had been ripped off, a cow came and slept on my saree; Meharaju and Asiyat Jameela who looked at that keep teasing me. They call me as 'the philanthropist who gave her saree to a cow.'"

Kalam too mocked her, "Hey! This seems to be a great title." The day went by. Abdul Kalam left the next day for his job. With the passage of time, people were slowly recovering from the impact made by the storm. The government and NGOs gave relief to those affected by the storm.

Electricity was given to Jain Maraikayar and Chinna Maraikka's houses. The Pamban Bridge was rebuilt and rail transportation resumed from March 1, 1965.

A sore that had developed on Jain Maraikayar's leg worsened. He found it difficult to walk. They tried different treatments. Abdul Kalam wanted to take him to Chennai for treatment. His father refused.

Time flew. The temple festivities began. For some unknown reason, the usual honours given to the Jain Maraikayar family was stopped. After consulting his lawyer, Chinna Maraikka said that they should present their case in court. Jain Maraikayar who was patiently listening to his son replied, "You want me to file a complaint against Ramanathaswamy? No need for all that. Let's just leave it as such." He stopped his son from filing a formal complaint.

Jain Maraikayar, now with a white beard and sharp eyes, lay motionless inside his house for nearly two years; his son Mustafa Kamal took care of him. After performing her 'Maghrib' prayer, his eldest daughter-in-law visited Jain Maraikayar in his house everyday. If she missed visiting him even once, he would send word for her. Chinna Maraikka who normally came to see Jain Maraikayar after praying didn't come one day. He asked for the reason. His other son replied, "Kaakka has a fever."

Jain Maraikayar immediately came to visit his son Chinna Maraikka along with his other son on a horse cart. Chinna Maraikka felt sad that his father had to come all the way in spite of his old age. Since Ahmed Kanima became their daughter-in-law at a very young age, she became an expert cook. Her father-in-law loved the tea she prepared. He ordered her to send the morning tea, along with his breakfast, lunch and dinner. Ahmed Kanima prepared various delicacies for him and sent them to him.

One day, as per her father-in-law's request, she prepared his favourite 'fish avial'. Chinna Maraikka, who had left for his afternoon prayer, came to her and said, "Father is unable to eat anything." She came to visit her father-in-law. He asked her to be seated.

He recited "la ilaha illa Allah..." amidst panting breaths and died. Upon hearing about his father's demise, Abdul Kalam rushed home. The life of the 102-year-old great man, who had shouldered many responsibilities in his family came to an end. His sons did his last rites as prescribed in Islam; they recited the Holy Qur'an for forty days and did the Duwah for his eternal peace. They prepared rice and curry, recited the Fatiha, and served the food to all their friends and relatives. They also served the needy.

'Sahan' is a huge porcelain plate. (In 'One Sahan', four people could eat and in 'Half Sahan', two people could eat. They prepare milk rice and 'dhuvai' and serve it on these plates. The Maraikayar family possessed several such 'Sahans.') 'Dhuvai' is a sweet mentioned in the fortieth day Fatiha recitation. Raw rice has to be soaked in water. After draining it out, it was ground to a flour in a mortar. The flour is then fried lightly and sieved. It would then be partitioned into 21, 23, 25 and 27 measures. On the night before, they mixed 4 scraped coconuts, 4 eggs, and one measure of sugar. They heated the mixture of coconut milk, sugar, eggs and flour in a stove till it attained a creamy texture and added cardamom powder, paneer, kishmish, cashews and ghee and placed it in Sahans which were served the following day to everyone.

Jain Maraikayar insisted that we should never address anyone as a 'beggar.' He preferred to use the term 'Musafir' which meant 'passerby.' Several musafirs were served during the last rites of Jain Maraikayar. Many people came for the ceremony. Prayers for his eternal peace were done.

Since people referred to Chinna Maraikayar fondly as 'Maraikka', we too shall do so in this book.

As Maraikka was recounting past memories about his father, he was thinking about 'Salna(fish gravy).' Jain Maraikayar never shouted at beggars; one day, an old man asked for food; even before he was served food, he shouted 'Salna'; Jain Maraikayar laughed and said, "Food goes with Salna, right?". He then brought them from Ahmed Kanima and served him food on one plate and Salna on another.

From that day onwards, the beggar always came to their house and asked for food with Salna; he came to be referred to as 'Salna' in their house. Even if he didn't come for one day to their house, Jain Maraikayar would become upset. One day, as he left to pray in the morning, he saw a figure curled up in a blanket in the pial opposite their house. "Who are you?" he enquired to which the fellow replied, "Salna." He then left to pray. He asked his daughter-in-law for hot water and tea. He also went to wake Salna before drinking his tea.

Salna was old and weak; he couldn't roam about to get food; however, Jain Maraikayar took that responsibility; every time before eating, he would offer water, food and Salna to the man and then only consume his food. He had strictly instructed that he should not be served with the previous day's leftover food. When people asked him for a reason, he replied, "One should consume food within four hours of its preparation; it loses all nutrients after that time." He made sure that non-consumable food was never served to the musafirs.

If he heard anyone begging from outside, he rushed with food. He always insisted that food and gravy should be served in separate containers. His habits were also environmentally-friendly. In Rameswaram, they sprinkled water normally to put Kolams outside the house. However, right from his childhood, in order to get rid of the dust, Jain Maraikayar sprinkled water outside his house. This became a regular habit.

Asiyamma was dejected after her husband's death; during the time of the Iddah itself, her body and mind became weak. Her granddaughters who remembered the kindness of their Vappamma when they were young, now assisted her during her old age. They took good care of Asiyamma.

Everyday, they gave her a bath, made her wear fresh clothes, and prepared different food varieties. They conversed on various topics to lighten her up.

Asiyamma addressed her grandson as 'Prince' since his name was also Jainulabdeen which was her husband's name. The granddaughters would make fun of her. Occasionally, during holidays, Abdul Kalam would come home to visit his mom; they all would sit around Asiyamma and converse.

It would appear as if she was listening to them intently; if she was asked any question, she would give a crisp reply; Asiyamma, who bought new clothes and stitched her own blouses, lost interest in everything. Her daughter-in-law Ahmed Kanima and her granddaughters took great care of her.

❑

Aerial Root - 4

The month of Ramadan and the festival of Ramzan were celebrated.

Asiya called out the name 'Kanima' and rushed to the backyard. She was Jain Maraikayar's brother's wife Alima Amma's sister; therefore, the children of Chinna Maraikka would address her also as 'Vappamma.' Her speech will be filled with jokes; she was an expert in hand medicine and checking the pulse. She would also explain these through simple steps to people.

She usually visited in the evening and asked, "What are you making for the night?" That day, since she had come in the afternoon, everyone was surprised. The granddaughters welcomed her. Maraikka who was sitting inside welcomed his Chachi. Asiya's house was to the left of the Maraikayar's house; as she wanted to visit her daughter Muthu Qureshi, she had stepped outside her house; then her eyes fell upon a tiger beetle stuck in Maraikayar's house door.

In case Maraikayar left for his afternoon 'Dhuhr' prayer, he had to go through that door. Since the tiger beetle was poisonous, she had come there to inform them. Maraikayar came through the backyard with a stick, to the front portion of his house. After he killed the insect, he asked them to clean his house.

As he left to perform his 'Dhuhr' prayer, all his thoughts were about his kind Asiya Chachi. After thanking God during his prayer, he also did Duwah for his beloved Asiya Chachi to keep her well.

As time went by, Asiyamma became fragile and weak; in spite of his rigorous work hours, Abdul Kalam would visit his mother; he would summon physicians and doctors and buy the medicines prescribed by them for his mother. Asiyamma was bed-ridden; her eldest daughter-in-law and granddaughters took good care of her; Abdul Kalam had come to see his mother; Alithambi Ravuthar's son Alauddin Ravuthar from the Modiyar house had come as always to enquire about Asiyamma's health. He asked Kalam, "How is your mom now? Your mother is a kind woman; she has donated to so many people; ask her to donate money to a few people as charity; Allah will ease her pain then." They listened to Alauddin uncle's advice. They kept some money under Asiyamma's people for donation.

Since Asiyamma knew people who were poor, whenever they came to see her, she would give them some money from under her pillow. Everyone blessed her for her kindness. Lunch was being prepared; Kanima plucked a snake gourd from her house garden for preparing the curry. She started to peel its skin; her hands were working while her thoughts recalled fond memories of her beloved father-in-law Jain Maraikayar; he was fond of snake gourd; he would ask her to cook it with fish for the curry. At times, he asked her to prepare it with scraped coconut without adding any masala; Kanima was recalling the way in which he used to instruct her now; "Please cook snake gourd so that its green colour doesn't change", he would say to her. Kanima passionately recalled the way in which he instructed her to prepare the delicacies.

Sultan Maraikayar's son Ibrahim Maraikayar who had left soon after his wife's death, visited his hometown from Silabad with his young wife and children. He had come to visit Periyappa's daughter and his elder sister Asiyamma; "Ratha! Ratha!" he cried and held her hand tightly. Asiyamma opened her eyes when she realised that someone was touching her hand. She smiled at him; they both perhaps recalled their past incidents looking at one another. Asiyamma seemed to be content; she closed her eyes and slept. Ibrahim Maraikayar, who sat beside his beloved sister left late at night from their house.

The next morning, he visited his sister's daughter Asim Zohara; they recalled their childhood pranks together; they discussed the way they played and how they fought as children; he conveyed his condolences for her husband's loss. Asim Zohara's Iddah period was over. He therefore asked her to visit her mom Asiyamma.

That evening, Asim Zohara accompanied by her brothers Mustafa Kamal and Kasim Mohammed visited her elder brother Chinna Maraikka's house to be with her mother. Maraikka, Kanima and their children made them sit beside Asiyamma; she opened her eyes partially and saw that her four children, daughter-in-law, grandson and granddaughters were beside her; when her daughter called her 'Umma', she just responded 'Um'; 'Look over here, Ratha has come", said her sons. She saw her daughter and once again closed her eyes.

The three brothers who had seen their beloved eldest sister clad in Koranad silk sarees and jewellery all the time encountered her for the first time clad in all white dress after her husband's death. They felt sorry for her loss. "This is all Allah's wish!" They tried to pacify themselves and greeted their sister warmly. Ahmed Kanima asked her sister-in-law to stay with them for a while; she therefore spent the night in her brother's house. She and Kanima were awake throughout the night. They both kept watch on Asiyamma. The next morning, with her sons, daughter and daughter-in-law beside her, Asiyamma breathed her last.

They informed Abdul Kalam immediately; their near and dear ones had also arrived. Asiyamma's siblings were no more. During her final days, she felt their loss greatly. She always lamented. She used to say, "What do I need? None of my brothers are alive? Even my Chacha's son Ibrahim is in Silabad which is far away!"

Perhaps, in order to reduce her strain, Ibrahim Maraikayar visited her during her last days. Their family members said to one another, "This was Allah's wish perhaps; the brother got a glimpse of his beloved sister during her final days!"

Since Abdul Kalam had informed that he would come by the night train, they prepared for her death ceremony; In Maiyavaadi, Pambai Kanna's son Iburamsa was digging the ground for burial. (Since he wouldn't comb his hair properly and tied it in a clumsy manner, he was known as Pambai. Kanna means granny. She and her husband belonged to the town 'PeriyaPattinam'; since her father-in-law had gone to Colombo for earning, they were there for a while before coming to Rameswaram; their son Iburamsa was a honest man with a stiff and steady body; he was an expert cook; during the Ramadan month, he used to be the head cook for preparing the porridge; he also dug the ground for Mayyith; he took this as an assignment; he was allowed to enter inside Maraikayar's house and maintained good relationship with the.) Guests who had come from outside for the Mayyith were made to stay in the opposite houses which belonged to Jain Maraikayar; upma and coffee were prepared and served. Mustafa Kamal had gone to the railway station to pick up Abdul Kalam; he came with Kalam at midnight.

His siblings hugged Kalam and cried uncontrollably at the loss of their beloved mother; Asiyamma was bathed and preparations for her burial began. That night, surrounded by Petromax lamps, her final procession happened.

Asiyamma's body was buried in Mohideen Andavar Mosque's Maiyavaadi burial ground. That was the end of a great legend who took huge responsibility in uplifting her family amidst chaos.

Abdul Kalam, who was busy with his space research project, left the same day.

He asked his elder brother to perform the last rites for his mother; he arranged for the recitation of the Holy Qur'an for forty days followed by the Duwah for her eternal peace. On the third, seventh and fifteenth day, Fatiha was recited; on all forty days, Fatiha was recited and sweets and fruits served to everyone. Her granddaughters greatly missed their granny; they looked at her bed, her sarees, her 'Tasbih' and all her belongings with desperation. They recalled how Vappamma loved to read the 'Kalkandu' magazine and how she said 'TamilVaanan' as 'Tamulvaan' and how they used to mock her for that.

'Qur'anin Kural' is a magazine that preaches the edicts of the Holy Qur'an to Tamil muslims. Maraikayar bought this and read it. When the publisher of this magazine had come to Rameswaram to introduce it, he developed a friendship with Jain Maraikayar. That was Allah's wish! This trend continued for generations. Alhaj A. M. Abdul Jaffar Bhagavi's message was conveyed to everyone in the family: "Please do not travel to uninhabited places during night time."

Solar eclipse was about to happen; Jain Maraikayar's family knew well about eclipses; on the day before the eclipse, they would bring 'Arugampul' (a type of grass) and put them inside flour jars and drinking water; at the time of the eclipse, they never kept any cooked food; they always ate well before the eclipse. Even infants were not fed with food and water. "At the time of the eclipse, drinking water and eating food are prohibited", they informed their children.

They performed the Wudu ritual and prayed during the eclipse time; till the time of the end of the eclipse, they performed the Duwah. Be it day or night, once the eclipse got over, all members of the family had to take a bath; only after that, they prepared fresh food to eat.

Abdul Kalam, who was busy with his space research work, successfully launched SLV-3 rocket and Rohini satellite and earned great name and fame. He was awarded the 'Padma Bhushan' in 1981 for his achievements. His family members were proud of his 'Padma' award and achievements.

Time went by swiftly. Asim Zohara's health deteriorated; they tried all sorts of medication to cure her. But it was of no use. One night, she left this world, leaving her only daughter behind. Her siblings, friends and relatives buried her body and prayed for her soul to rest in peace.

❑

Aerial Roots - 5, 6

Maraikka's elder daughter Thangarani's only daughter Zohara Begum's marriage was fixed; they were looking for a suitable match for her son Sarbuddin as well; elder sister and younger brother got married on the same day. The following year, Sarbuddin became the father of Nilofer Kurshid. The Maraikka-Ahmed Kanima couple felt happy to witness the birth of the first child of their fourth generation.

At that time, Abdul Kalam was busy with the missile project for India. The news was conveyed to him. Abdul Kalam, who built the Trishul and the Prithvi missiles, also dedicated the 'Agni' missile for national security. He was awarded several titles and honours for his contribution to his motherland; his siblings were proud of their brother. His near and dear ones appreciated him. Kasim Mohammed, who was born before Abdul Kalam passed away unexpectedly; his elder brothers and Kalam lamented over his loss.

Next, his 'Akash' missile hit the sky.

One day, Ahmed Kanima finished all her household chores as always. She bathed, fed the Maraikayar children, and ate; after her evening 'Asr' prayer, she sat on the porch outside the house and asked for 'Varamalar' magazine as it was a Sunday; 'I have completed everything", she said and kept the book down; she probably knew her fate already! She then completed her 'Maghrib' and 'Isha' prayers and sat down on the prayer mat; as she noticed her husband leaving for the mosque for the 'Isha' prayer, she tried to get up to prepare dinner; she couldn't get up. She asked her daughter-in-law to fetch her husband.

Even then, her daughter Nazema couldn't understand her mother's condition. She asked her mom, "What's the matter?" Maraikka had completed his 'Isha' prayer. As he saw his daughter-in-law's shadow lurking behind him, he enquired to her, "What happened?" She replied, "Aunt asked me to fetch you." He made his wife lie down on his lap. He asked her, "What is the matter?" She was unable to speak a word. Kanima looked at her husband, daughter, daughter-in-law and grandchildren and closed her eyes.

The doctor was summoned; by the time their family doctor Kalilur Rahman arrived, Kanima's brothers, brother's wives, and their children had reached there. The doctor checked her pulse and confirmed the news of her death. The lady, who had come at a very young age as the daughter-in-law to the Maraikayar family, and who had participated in all their family rituals by leading the way, had breathed her last. Words cannot describe the loss of such a person! Maraikka couldn't believe that his life partner had left him once and for all. His uncle's daughter Arulmozhi Rani told him, "Uncle, keep the body down." He kept the body of his beloved life that was on his lap, down. He sat down in the front hall. When people enquired of her death, he said, "My wife was a pious woman. After finishing her prayer, she waited for me to finish mine, before leaving this world." Not once did Kanima complain of illness. She shouldered all the responsibilities of the Maraikayar family. She meant the world to them. Her husband and children couldn't bear this loss and cried uncontrollably.

Abdul Kalam wrote in his letter: “My Machi took care of me as I grew up.” He participated in the fifteenth day’s Fatiha and pacified his brother.

As per his request, the Holy Qur’an was recited for forty days and the final rites were performed. During the funeral procession of T.S. Mohammed Maraikayar’s only daughter Ahmed Kanima, all relatives from their family participated. Kanima treated everyone equally. Everyone missed this great lady. People from many different places enquired of her death.

In 1997, Kalam was awarded the 'Bharat Ratna.' At the time Kalam was the Chairman of DRDO and the Scientific Adviser to the Defence Ministry. He had invited his elder brother Chinna Maraikka, grandsons, and Kasim Mohammed's son-in-law Nizamuddin for the event. In his heart, Maraikka silently thanked his parents and grandmother Hasanachiyar for all their contribution towards Kalam's growth and development.

Abdul Kalam and his achievements had become world famous. When people got to know that Kalam's birth place was Rameswaram, the abode of Ramanathaswamy, they flocked to his house. In order to distinguish his house from others, the house was named as 'HOUSE OF KALAM'.

The Tamil people were proud of Kalam's participation in the Pokhran nuclear bomb test explosions in 1998. In 1999, Kalam became a Cabinet Minister as he was appointed as the Principal Scientific Adviser to the Indian government.

Thangarani's son Zakir Hussain got married to Vannangundu Saburnisa.

Kalam hosted his elder brother Chinna Maraikka while he was working in Thiruvananthapuram, Hyderabad, and

Delhi. Kalam enjoyed being with his brother. Abdul Kalam worked in the central government's department of research for 43 years and retired. He then worked as a Professor in Anna University, Chennai as per their request.

Kalam arranged for a telephone connection in 'HOUSE OF KALAM'. He used to chat with his brother Chinna Maraikka over the phone. He informed Chinna Maraikka that he would be joining as a faculty member in Anna University, Chennai post-retirement. When Chinna Maraikka heard this, he prayed to God, "Please let my brother get whatever he wishes for! Make him progress!"

Kaakka's Duwah was heard by Allah! Abdul Kalam became the eleventh President of India in 2002. He had invited his family members for the oath-taking ceremony. His elder brother, accompanied by 35 family members from paternal and maternal sides, went to attend the function in Delhi. When Abdul Kalam took oath as the Indian President, tears of joy poured out from Maraikka's eyes. He thanked Allah for his mercy.

People in Rameswaram celebrated him as 'The President's brother'. There were celebrations all around. Their house was lit with joy and festivities.

In 2006, Abdul Kalam sent his Kaakka, along with Kaakka's daughter Nazema and grandson Ghulam to Haj pilgrimage. They visited the holy places of Mecca and Medina and completed their Haj pilgrimage. They did

Duwah for Kalam's well-being and thanked Allah for his mercy.

Summer vacation began; following the invitation sent by his brother Kalam, Maraikka went for Delhi along with his all his relatives (starting from his eldest son Shahul Hameed all the way up till Kasim Mohammed's son Jahubar along with their families); 56 people were there in the tour. Each of their families were allotted separate rooms inside the Rashtrapati Bhavan. Different delicacies were served to them. They went to Ajmer Dargah to do the Jiyarat (Doing Duwah to Allah for the eternal peace of Islamic prophets). Kalam sent money in separate envelopes to all of them. It will take several pages to write about President Abdul Kalam's hospitality. While we were in Rashtrapati Bhavan, he made us recite the 'Maghrib' prayer followed by the Duwah together; he encouraged everyone.

In the Mughal Garden of Rashtrapati Bhavan he honoured his family's Hajis and also celebrated his dear brother's birthday. Lights were flashed during the night and they all shared their Haj pilgrimage experience. They were all given the Holy Qur'an as gifts. Kalam had arranged for a scrumptious dinner that night.

It was now time for all of us to leave the Rashtrapati Bhavan; everyone felt grateful to Kalam for his hospitality. This was a once-in-a-lifetime experience for all of us... each of us were given a shawl and a basket of fruits while departing the place. Such was Kalam's hospitality!

Only Abdul Kalam could have done all this! His secretaries Shri. Prasad, Mr. Sheridon, and Mr. Ponraj and other Rashtrapati Bhavan officials took great care of all our needs.

After reaching Chennai Egmore railway station, Shahul Hameed, his wife and daughter departed from there to reach Bangalore. Everyone bid their farewell. But no one could predict the future at the time! None of us knew that we were never going to see Shahul Hameed anymore! He clasped his father's hands, bid goodbye to sister Nazema and left the train waving at them.

He died the following month; Chinaappa Abdul Kalam asked grandson Sheikh Dawood who was working in Bangalore at the time, to leave with his periyappa's body. He was accompanied by his Periyamma and Ratha for Rameswaram. At a ripe old age, Maraikka had lost his son! Thoughts of his son's birth at a very young age and their struggles in bringing him up crossed his mind.

Vappa Jainulabdeen was fond of his first grandson Shahul Hameed; He would fill a bucket of water everyday and give him a bath; he would also dry his grandson's clothes; the Maraikayar family had lost their most cherished grandson! Friends and relatives came from all over the world.

People who got to know that Abdul Kalam's brother's son Shahul Hameed's corpse was in the train from Bangalore to Rameswaram paid their respects to him at every station. The District Governor and the Superintendent of Police laid flower rings on behalf of the government and paid their respects.

"Just like his mom Ahmed Kanima, Shahul Hameed also left this world without much suffering", everyone said. Shahul Hameed's body was buried in Rameswaram Mohideen Abdul Kadhar Andavar mosque's Maiyavaadi burial ground.

Akin to Paventhar's verses: "With the rotation of the sun, the days passed by one after the other..."

In 2006, Nazema got her doctorate degree form Madurai Kamaraj University.

❑

Aerial Root - 7

Thangarani's son Sarbuddin's daughter Nilofer Kurshid got married to Hajat Yousif in Thangachi Matam. Maraikka intertwined their hands and blessed the couple. On April 25, 2008, 'Hanija' was born as the fifth-generation member of the Maraikka, Abdul Kalam family. People belonging to Nilofer's earlier generation were all younger than her. However, Hanija addressed them all as grandpa and grandma.

"Our grandson has got a granddaughter", the grandfathers announced proudly.

Maraikka who had been narrating the story told her, "This is the story of our family tree. I pray to God that this family tree should continue to grow for generations to come. Ameen." He opened up his palms and prayed to Allah.

Let the aerial roots grow...!

Let our country prosper...!

❑